I0445861

The Secret Ladder

Trail Creek Press
Copyright © 2012 J.S. Tyndall
All rights reserved.

ISBN: 0-6156-0033-6
ISBN-13: 9780615600338

This is a work of fiction. Names, characters, places and incidents either
are the product of the author's imagination or are used fictitiously. Any
resemblance to actual persons, living or dead, is entirely coincidental.

# The Secret Ladder

## A Novel

## J.S. Tyndall

Trail Creek Press
2012

On a dark night, Kindled in love with yearnings—oh, happy chance! -

I went forth without being observed, My house being now at rest.

In darkness and secure, By the secret ladder, disguised—oh happy chance!—

In darkness and concealment, My house being now at rest.

...In secret, when none saw me,

Nor I beheld aught, Without light or guide, save that which burned in my heart.

—from the poem, Dark Night (of the Soul)
Attributed to St. John of the Cross
Early 17th Century

For my mother
Laurie,
In loving memory

# 1

The rain had stopped during the night. As Sarah Coleman drove north of Santa Barbara, past Goleta and the State beaches—El Capitan, Refugio, Gaviota—her thoughts turned to David. This weekend visit to see friends in El Encanto was meant to coincide with the one year anniversary of his death and to mark the passage of time.

There was to be no unveiling of the gravestone after the traditional twelve months of mourning for there was no stone. David's ashes, poured from the small urn the mortuary had given her, were already mingled with the earth, the wind, gone. She and Julie had scattered them a few weeks after his death— weeks after the memorial service at Mt. Sinai was over—in the hills above Refugio, in sight of the ocean. It was not the hardest thing Sarah had ever done; it had been harder to watch him die, to give him permission to abandon her. He was too young to die at 46, a year older than Sarah and she was too young to be a widow. The word itself frightened her; it sounded black, hollow, permanent. During their last days together she clung to his thin, afflicted body. She did not let him go easily and in the end he had to beg her and she regretted that she had been selfish.

That day, like this one, was clear and cold, wet from recent rains that left traces of a Mediterranean winter. The hills had turned green seemingly overnight. The spindly mustard and purple lupine were already beginning to show in places and California poppies punctuated the edges of the Coast Highway in bright, orange bunches. She and David had always wanted to go to the real Mediterranean.

As she and Julie sprinkled what was left of him, this powdery ash, Sarah thought she would lose her footing—and her mind—and not be able to stand. The chaparral grew blurry as she had tried to see past it to the sparkling Pacific. Mother and daughter held each other and cried, for once putting their singular losses aside and coming together for David's sake and for their own. Sarah had wanted to remember everything about that day. She had not invited anyone else to join them. Friends and family had attended the memorial service at Hillside—even Claire, Sarah's mother, came with her caregiver, Asya. Becca, Sarah's sister, flew in with her husband Andrew. David's younger brother Adam sat with their distraught parents who traveled from Boca Raton. But Sarah had chosen to separate this private ceremony for a reason. This was between her and David and their only child. She could not have borne the inevitable words about moving on. Even now, a year later, she didn't know what they meant—only that something in her life had to change if she was to save it.

❧❧

Sarah called Julie from the car. It was after noon in New York.

"Hello?" Julie said sleepily.

"Did I wake you? I'm sorry, sweetheart," Sarah said.

"It's OK. I need to get up," Julie said.

"I wanted to let you know I'm on my way to spend the weekend with Sharon and Russell. Do you want their number?"

"Not really."

"It's so beautiful. I'm driving past Refugio. Remember?"

"Do I *remember*?"

Sarah swallowed but didn't respond. Why was it so difficult to talk to Julie, to find the right words?

"It's February in New York and I think it's supposed to snow today."

"Right," said Sarah. "How are you?"

"The show is in rehearsals. It's amazing. My part is small, you know, not a speaking part. But the chorus is in every number so I get to sing a lot. And the people I work with are awesome."

"It's a 70's era thing, isn't that what you told me?" Sarah searched her brain for the details of the off-off Broadway musical.

"Yeah. Nothing you've ever heard of but I think you'd like it. You gonna come to Opening Night? It's in three weeks."

Sarah pictured her calendar. There was the trip to San Diego on Wednesday, the open house the following weekend—she would have to see if Maya could help get the place ready for it. And—oh damn—she'd forgotten to call Jean Bartlett before she left to give her a key. Jean was her real estate broker. Then there was the Alumnus of the Year award dinner coming up at the end of March, and the dread Weingold proposal. At least she would bring the materials for the proposal with her and start on the outline at Sharon's.

"I'll try, honey," answered Sarah, distracted. Her car swerved to the right and she was startled by the sound of the rumble strips at the edge of the shoulder. "Things are a little crazy around here, but..."

Julie interrupted her. "Daddy wouldn't have missed it."

The subtext.

"I'll really try," said Sarah.

# 2

The Starbuck's in Montecito was always crowded. Sarah had stopped for coffee on the way back from El Encanto. She stood outside—the sun warm on her back—and stretched her legs. She called Asya, a tall woman in her 60's who was her mother's Bulgarian caregiver, to make plans to see Claire.

"You come here for dinner tomorrow night? I make Moussaka!" said Asya with enthusiasm. Company, Sarah guessed. Asya wanted her to spend time with them; so much time alone with Claire couldn't be an easy job.

"I won't be able to leave work before five."

"5:30 then. We eat 5:30. It's OK?" asked Asya who routinely had salad on the table for Claire an hour earlier.

"I'll try." That seemed to be her default answer lately.

"Good. You want talk to Claire?" asked Asya. "I go get her."

"Sure."

"I bring the phone." Sarah could hear Asya crossing the entry hall that separated the kitchen from the bedrooms. "Oh, Sarah, her eyes they are closed. You want I wake her?"

"No, let her rest."

"Yes, OK. I see you tomorrow."

"Good bye, Asya," Sarah said, sighing deeply once Asya hung up, thinking of what else she needed to do once she got home.

As Sarah turned up the driveway she examined her house, a small 50's ranch on a wide lot, a "For Sale" sign at the edge of the driveway.

Sarah dropped her things in the living room and played her messages. The first was from Julie.

"Hi, it's me," Julie said with a downward inflection (she had sounded almost happy the other day). "Call me when you get home, OK? Hope you had fun with your friends." Cool, sarcastic.

Sarah would put that one off until later. There was a message from Becca, in Chicago. There were two calls from Jean asking about showings over the weekend. Sarah dialed her number, reaching her in the car.

"Where have you *been?*" asked Jean.

"I meant to call you and give you a key, I'm sorry," said Sarah. I was away for the weekend.

"If you'd *told* me I could have shown it to several people while you were gone. Oh well, there's plenty of daylight left," said Jean. "I have a listing appointment I'm going to now. I'd like to reach this woman who called the office after driving by the house. I could meet her around four-thirty. Would that work for you?"

Sarah walked with the phone in her hand through the kitchen and looked around—not too bad, just a few things in the sink. She walked into the bedroom. She would have to put fresh towels in the bath—that was it.

"I guess it'd be all right," Sarah said, wondering when she was ever going to get to the Weingold proposal. The seller always had to disappear when there were showings. She could take her work down to the Coffee Bean on Ventura and Oakdale.

"Great. I'll get back to you."

Sarah sat at the Coffee Bean and tried to focus on work but could not. She'd brought the old Ford proposal to see how it could be tweaked and revised for Weingold. Glancing at the clock over the counter she wondered when the showing would be over. Sarah felt something slip. She'd been holding on tight to all the pieces in her life but all at once, waiting for the call from Jean something slipped and she felt one step closer to losing it all. "You can go home now—she's gone," Jean said when she finally called. There was a siren in the background. Sarah heard the same siren as a fire engine weaved around cars on the Boulevard.

"What did she say?" asked Sarah, gathering her papers.

"She said it was missing a bedroom, but we knew that."

It's missing more than a bedroom, thought Sarah, and what was lacking couldn't be measured in square feet.

She managed two hours of work at the dining room table before realizing how hungry she was. The proposal wasn't going to be as difficult as she'd feared. Typical of her to get overly anxious before starting a project. She could do a lot of cutting and pasting and then the relevant faculty would have their input. It would be a respectable length and she might even have a very rough draft if she was able to stay awake long enough to squeeze in another couple of hours this evening.

She thought about the meal the night before at Sharon and Russell's—the warmth of their home—the ease of their marriage. She reached into the refrigerator for some Jarlsberg, sliced a tomato and made a grilled-cheese sandwich in the toaster oven.

It was chilly in the house. While she waited for the cheese to melt she walked across the living room to turn up the thermostat. It was the contrast, she supposed, between her life now and how it had been. She didn't want to dwell on it. It was six-thirty and dark. The hour was a relief to her. She was grateful for the shortened days of winter. They promised long evenings of limited demands. Her loneliness would evolve into something softer, knowing it would end in sleep.

# 3

A copper bank of elevators mirrored the figures of young professionals sipping coffee, talking basketball scores, and reviewing documents. A UPS man in brown shorts held packages and overnight envelopes marked URGENT. Sarah Coleman and Dean John Carver of Kelton Hall waited with them, the muscles in Sarah's face tensed in anticipation of the day ahead.

The express elevator whisked them to the top floor and sumptuous reception area of Mahoney and Michaels, the oldest and most prestigious law firm in Los Angeles.

A petite woman with neat gray hair ushered them into Walter Blakely's corner office. Blakely, a large man in his late 60's, was buttoning his tight fitting, expensive suit jacket as they walked in. The four of them shook hands. Tall and willowy, Sarah smiled at Walter and commented on the view. It was one of those clear winter days downtown when you could see over the Harbor Freeway to the high-rises in Century City and the flat squares of buildings all the way to the Pacific. She could make out jets taking off from LAX. Sarah wished she were someplace else, say, on a plane to Paris.

"So how's the Campaign coming along?" asked Walter, sitting down behind his desk.

Sarah sat next to the dean in one of twin leather armchairs. Luckily, this first question was not hers to answer. The dean leaned forward and faced Blakely, one of the school's most accomplished alumni—a corporate litigator and senior partner at Mahoney for years, still pulling down seven figures, still handling the big cases. She quietly anticipated John Carver's speech.

"Frankly, Walt, it's a challenge, a real challenge. As you know, the consultants didn't think we could do it but we're giving it our best effort. The state funded portion of this project is not going to get any easier. If we don't raise enough on the private side, it could go away entirely. It's a tricky thing—raising this much money from such a young law school. But we have to do it, Walt, and we're here to ask for your help."

Sarah had hoped Carver would name an amount but he didn't. He rarely did. It was his biggest problem as a fundraiser—he couldn't make 'the ask.' He let the prospect determine the size of the gift. Sarah looked to see what Blakely would say, mentally preparing her own response in case the number was too low, planning how to save the meeting.

"I reviewed the list of gift opportunities you sent me, Sarah," said Blakely fingering some papers on his desk. "Lilly and I discussed it and we have decided to donate $50,000." Blakely sat back and smiled. Sarah half expected him to recline in his chair with his hands behind his head and cross his feet up on the desk.

The dean looked at Sarah who didn't return the glance but steadied her gaze on Walter.

"$50,000 is a wonderful gift, a generous gift," Sarah said, "for most people."

Walter, basking in the recognition of his largesse, registered a double take.

"The other alums are looking to you, Walter—your associates, the younger partners, your peers at the other big firms. Kelley, Hanson. Gould and Gould. There aren't many of our alums who've accomplished what you have. We'd like you to think about a larger gift, a two hundred and fifty thousand dollar commitment. I mean, Walter," with this she looked over at the dean who was examining some lint on his trousers, "if not you, then who?"

Walter eyed Sarah. "A quarter of a million? You should have been a lawyer," he said.

He walked them to the elevators, past the row of desks and file cabinets and busy secretaries; nodding to younger partners and associates along the way. "I'll give it some more thought and let you know," he said, reaching his paw of a hand to push the "Down" button.

"When did you decide to do *that*?" Dean Carver inquired of Sarah once the doors closed and they were alone.

Sarah pressed her fingers to her temples. "I'm not sure," she said. "Did I go too far?"

"Hell no!" Carver said. "Blakely thinks you're terrific."

The buzzer on Sarah's office phone sounded.

"It's Jean Bartlett, said her assistant, a testy, large young woman who was new and still on probation. "She says it's important."

"Thanks, Tania."

Sarah punched her line. "Hi Jean," she said, her jaw tightening.

"You haven't returned my calls," started Jean. "You're acting like you don't care whether you sell this house or not."

"Of course I do," Sarah lied, for at that moment she could have forgotten about the whole thing—that is if it weren't for the money. "It's just that tomorrow I leave for San Diego. I meant to tell you I'd be gone for a few days and there's a lot to do here before I go."

"We have an offer coming in tonight," said Jean, sounding impatient.

"Really…" Sarah felt unbalanced. I thought your message said something about a price reduction."

"That's true. I was going to suggest it. I'm not sure what the offer is, it might be way below your asking price but their broker says it's very clean. I met the buyers today at the showing. They're a nice young couple. She grew up in the neighborhood. Her grandmother lives a half mile away. Seems like a good fit."

'The buyers'—Sarah's head felt light. "What time did you want to come to the house? I'm having an early dinner with my mother."

"Eight? It shouldn't take long."

"I can be home by eight." Sarah felt her chest tighten. This had been happening lately.

ॐॐ

Claire waited at the end of the hall on the twelfth floor of her building. A big grin spread across her face when she saw Sarah get off the elevator and the hug she gave her daughter was long, *authentic*. Strange what the stroke had accomplished. Along with her verbal and cognitive abilities, it had wiped away any traces of coolness or hesitation from Claire's demeanor, leaving only a child's need for comfort and a child's inclination to love without restraint.

Asya appeared behind Claire looking pleased. The apartment smelled of fried meat and onions. Sara felt a little queasy but it was 5:30 and dinner was ready.

Claire's appetite was healthy though meals could present a challenge. Because of the stroke, she often—for example—confused her fork with her knife and, as she did this evening, used her fingers to pick up a pat of butter eating it a bite at a time.

"Mom," Sarah's stomach twisted into a knot at the sight of Claire's mistake, "put the butter down and use your knife instead. Here." Sarah showed her mother, who used to bake rolls, how to spread butter on one. Claire looked at Sarah with annoyance as if to say—I knew that! The knot in Sarah's stomach felt like a cold stone.

Sarah, Asya and Claire ate a quiet dinner. The apartment overlooked Palisades Park, a grassy strip lined with palm trees and frequented by joggers or retirees depending on the time of day. Claire checked her watch and got up—a paper napkin still tucked into her blouse—to turn the blinds just so. Sarah recalled how her mother used to enjoy watching the joggers early in the morning before they went to work. She didn't know if she paid attention to things like that any more. Claire turned around and waved to Sarah, as if asking for permission to be excused, and shuffled into her bedroom, her house slippers silent on the carpet. Sarah told Asya she needed to get home as well and went into the bedroom to kiss Claire goodbye.

The memory of the sale of their last house vividly returned to Sarah as she opened the front door. Jean Bartlett and a man in his late 40's, smelling of sweet aftershave and hairspray, moved into the living room. Sarah felt as though she was existing in the past and the present at once. The memory of that other night so filled the room that Sarah half expected David to walk in and begin the negotiations. She missed him. She missed a hundred things about him but right now she missed his business acumen and deal making expertise. Sarah walked into the kitchen.

"I started a pot of coffee," she explained, over her shoulder. Jean followed her.

"Larry told me the details on the way in. I think you're going to be happy with the offer."

Sarah reached for three mugs. She did not answer Jean but rather turned her head. The fast tears surprised her.

# 4

Sarah stopped at an old-fashioned coffee shop she liked, just off the 405, half-way to San Diego. It was known for its authentic Huevos Rancheros and she ordered them. She was starved. While she waited for her food, she opened the March issue of Bon Appetit. There would be time for work later, she rationalized. It was a souvenir issue on Provence. Sarah savored the photographs as well as the recipes—duck confit and a warm apple tart served in its baking dish, resting on a country farmhouse sideboard. Sarah imagined cooking this once she was home in her own kitchen. But she had just sold her kitchen.

She returned from the conference in San Diego to an inbox piled high with memos and messages and a calendar full of deadlines. She'd had enough down time between sessions and dinners to finish the Weingold proposal and was having Tania pull together some budget figures before presenting it to the Dean. She closed the door to her office and picked up the phone.

"Diane, it's Sarah."

"Are you O.K.?"

"Any chance you could meet me for coffee?"

"Now?"

"Impossible?"

"No—come over here—meet me at the Market Café."

Sarah felt a weight lift from her shoulders. She grabbed her purse and told Tania she'd be back soon with no added explanation.

Diane McCullough was the Associate Dean of the Well-bourne School of Management and a good work friend and colleague. Outside the building they gave each other a quick hug and went on to the Café. Diane was several years older than Sarah and had worked in the non-profit world for many years but was a relative newcomer to the University. She was a quick study and someone Sarah trusted.

"So?" Diane asked.

"I don't know—I have a lot of decisions to make right now and I could really use some help."

"Give me the list."

"Well first, I sold the house. We're in escrow—60 days—a week of which is almost over. It seems like it's going to go through so I need to find another place to live, among other things. My broker has some condos for me to look at in Studio City but I'm not sure. I may be ready for a change—a new job—something. There was a lot of interest from other institutions at the conference in San Diego—Virginia, Michigan—even Stanford.

Diane interrupted her. "You didn't tell me you were selling." She sipped her coffee. "OK," she began. "You've got too many things to think about here and one seems to hinge on the other. You need to prioritize. The house is a done deal, right?"

Sarah nodded.

Diane went on. "So you have to think about where you're going to live. I wouldn't take on too much change at once even though I think you're right about the law school—you've been there too long." She paused and looked out over the newly land-scaped business school courtyard. "You know, you could use some time to sort things out." Another pause. "I think you should ask

Carver for a leave of absence. A couple of months—the summer—say June and July."

Sarah's eyes opened wide. "Are we talking about the same John G. Carver, Wallace Professor of Law and Dean of Kelton Hall?"

Diane shrugged. "You're too valuable to lose. And if he does balk there will always be other jobs, especially with your track record. Talk to him. Call it a sabbatical for God's sake. You've put in a dozen years at Kelton—right?"

Sarah nodded. Time off—not to care for another person as she did for David and had been doing for Claire and Julie but time for herself.

"It sounds pretty indulgent," said Sarah. It had only been a fantasy—to travel, go back to France. See Paris again. Take a cooking class in Provence.

"What do you think?" asked Diane, checking her watch. "I have to go soon."

"I think you're the best," said Sarah smiling gratefully at her friend, feeling the crease on her forehead relax.

"It's worth a shot," said Diane standing up.

Sarah understood. Diane was urging her to bet on her own life.

Sarah went back to her office and called upstairs to make an appointment with the dean.

"*Today?*" Asked the Dean's assistant.

"It's personal," Sarah told her.

"He might have fifteen minutes after his 4 o'clock," the assistant said.

"That's fine. Thanks, Chang."

When the call came from the dean's office saying he would be available at 5:45, Sarah was relieved to know that she wouldn't have to wait another day, afraid she might lose her resolve.

At 5:30, the rest of the staff gone, Sarah cleaned up the piles on her desk and went in to the bathroom to comb her hair, brush her teeth and apply some lipstick. She walked up the stairs to the dean's office and took a deep breath before entering.

The dean's assistant was at her desk, typing something on her computer at warp speed. She looked up at Sarah who stood at her desk.

"Hi, Chang. Is he keeping you late again?"

"What do you think?" Answered Chang, a diminutive woman in her early thirties. At that moment the door to the dean's inner office opened and John Carver and two faculty members exited, laughing.

"Unbelievable," said one of them.

"Wait till Everett hears about this," said the other.

Above the sounds of their voices, John Carver said, "OK, Sarah. You've got ten minutes."

They sat at the dean's conference table. His windows overlooked a courtyard and garden where saucer magnolias and sycamores provided a quiet space for law students to study or grab coffee. Sarah had brought a pad and pen with her out of habit and laid them on the table. She clasped her hands in her lap and faced the dean.

"I've come to talk to you about a personal matter," Sarah began, hoping she wouldn't choke on her request. She wished she had some water.

"Chang told me."

Sarah looked squarely at Dean Carver. "I would like to take a leave this summer—from the middle of June to the middle of August. A—a sabbatical of sorts."

"Why?" the dean asked.

Sarah had not anticipated this simple question and paused before answering. Why? Diane had made it sound so plausible, so *logical*. Where was that logic now? What had she said—something about having 'time to sort things out'?

"I've just sold my house," she began. "I'm not sure where I want to move.

"What does this have to do with work? Sarah, you need to get to the point. I'm very busy."

Sarah drew herself upright in her chair. "You're right. OK. I feel I've been working very hard. Um, I just got back from San Diego where, uh…"

"Where what? Some other development types were asking questions? Making you offers?"

"This isn't about another job," said Sarah, swallowing hard, "it's—about me. I need some time away from work, time for myself. I would like to travel. Maybe take a class. I haven't made any plans yet. But this is a *good* time. The Campaign is going well. The alums are coming through. Now that Walter Blakely committed to $250,000 over five years he's leaning on Dick Rice at Gould and Gould. He says Rice makes more than he does plus his wife has money. Anyhow, things always slow down in the summer. I haven't taken a vacation since my husband died and—"

"Sarah, you did take several weeks off then. And it wasn't a good time either. A lot of people had to pick up the slack as I recall."

Hearing his recollection changed everything. Sarah asked if she could have a glass of water. He buzzed Chang who brought in two glasses. She took a few sips and with each one her fear seemed to dissolve and she sat a little straighter in her chair.

"I've been a good staff member, John. This is a great job and I'm lucky to have it."

"If I grant you the leave will you agree to stay through the end of the Campaign? Will you forget about any other job for the next year and a half until it's over?"

"I can't promise that but I have no plans to make any changes."

He got up from the table and went to his desk. Without a word he sorted through some papers. Then, he slid his suit jacket off the back of his chair and put it on.

"Is there anything else?" He asked.

"No, I guess that's it," said Sarah, standing, not knowing what to think. She slowly picked up her blank legal pad and pen and began to walk toward the door.

"Two months," he said, reaching for the phone. "Tell Personnel what you need and I'll sign the papers."

Sarah stopped, wanting to tell him how much she appreciated his understanding but he was already connected.

"Terry! I'm fine. How are <u>you</u>?" the dean inquired, smiling broadly as though the person on the other end of the line could see him. Then John Carver turned his back on Sarah.

# 5

A white truck pulled in front of the house in Woodland Hills. It was a cool Saturday morning in the middle of March as Sarah looked out the window past the birch trees in lime-green leaf, past the first of the old roses to show buds, and signed out of her e-mail program.

She watched a large man gather an armful of flattened cardboard boxes and walk up to the door

She met him in a flannel shirt, old khakis, and sheepskin slippers. She planned to begin packing as soon as he left.

"You're not the only one that's doing this, you know," he said, following Sarah into the living room. He was in his 50's with thinning mouse-brown hair and handed her his business card: Gary Firestone—Sales—Northridge Moving and Storage. "I mean puttin' your stuff away and seeing what's out there."

"I'm only storing my things because I haven't found another place to live." Sarah thought she sounded defensive.

He seemed not to hear. "We had one customer, much older than you, left her things with us for over two years. One day—and she pays us every month like clockwork—anyhow one day she calls and tells us to just get rid of it. Sell everything. She had twelve crates."

"Really?"

"Uh-huh. Tells me she's lived without all that garbage—that's what she called it, 'garbage'—for this long and she guesses she can do without it on a permanent basis."

Sarah looked around the room, at the bookshelves filled with the acquisitions of a lifetime. True, the wood furniture which included some very good antique reproductions was nicked in places and the sofa and two side chairs needed to be re-covered but they were still serviceable and moreover they were her *things*. There was the arm chair and ottoman for middle of the night reading, positioned beneath a standing lamp with a dimmer switch that would remind her it was hours before dawn and sleep was still possible. And there, hanging over a small bow front dresser, was the richly inked botanical print she and David bought together on a trip to San Francisco. David had been impatient with her indecision over framing the print and had eventually left the shop.

"That won't be me," Sarah said gesturing at the ladder-back chairs, the books, and their three or four good paintings. "All this is—was—a part of our life. I couldn't begin to replace it. By the way, did I mention escrow doesn't close until a few days after you move everything into storage? I'm nervous about the timing."

"Not a problem. Things usually work out," he said.

By the end of the weekend Sarah had managed to pack a half-dozen boxes. She had finished all the books in the living room and wrote the word "FRAGILE" in black marking pen across the side of a box of mementos. She had wrapped framed photographs in bubble wrap and tucked them one on top of the other with newspaper in between. There were family photos with boats or mountains in the background and larger group photos taken at various celebrations over the years. She picked up one of herself and a round-faced, dark-eyed man with dark brows and hair, his arm firmly clasped about her shoulder. They looked relaxed and happy. Sarah recalled when the picture was taken—in Hawaii on their fifteenth wedding anniversary. As she glanced down at her list of 'things to do' the print blurred. She sat cross-legged on the floor and began to cry, looking helplessly at the boxes and the bare shelves and her disassembled life.

She reached over and began frantically to pull apart one of the boxes labeled "CD's & Books." As she tossed several of the CD's out of the box, desperate to find what she was looking for, she came upon a bright yellow and blue colored cover—yellow and blue for sun and water. She placed the CD in the player and sat down to listen.

It was an album of slack key guitar music, bought on their final trip to Kauai, three months before David died. The doctors had concerns and told them what might come up while they were away, but David had insisted and Sarah went along with the idea.

They had stayed in their room with a view of the ocean for much of the week and had meals on the lanai as they watched the endless waves. She remembered thinking how much in love they still were after 23 years of marriage. Early in the marriage, she had been more critical of David (and he of her!). But the years had taught them about the give and take, the compromises that brought peace, how neither one was always right. They still had their moments, arguing about silly things, or, more often, about how to raise their daughter, but all that seemed long ago.

The recollection of that trip—the talks they'd had about Sarah's future, about Julie and all they hoped for her, surrounded by the remarkable beauty of the islands—pierced Sarah and touched the grief she held in a place deep inside. She sat among the boxes and repeated, "I can't do this, I can't do this." She wished she didn't have to go on, that she could just lie down and never get up again.

After some time, the emotion wrung out of her, Sarah went in and started water for a bath. She got out of her clothes and splashed water on her face and looked at herself briefly in the mirror. She wrapped a bath towel around her body and walked back to the living room. Lifting the bottle of Scotch that was David's from the silver tray that served as a dry bar, she carried it into the kitchen and poured a stiff drink. She sipped it slowly. The bitter-smooth liquid tasted right. She took it back to the bathroom along with the portable telephone. The hot water enveloped her as she slid downward. She took a long swallow, placing the glass on the porcelain edge of the tub, the alcohol already going to her head. She'd eaten only a bowl of soup for dinner and that had been hours ago. She closed her eyes and felt the steam on her face.

# 6

The phone rang. Had she dozed off? Startled and woozy from the Scotch and the bath, she reached for it.

"Hello?"

"Mom?" Julie's voice was mournful. Her breathing was erratic.

"Honey, it's so late. Are you OK?"

Was Julie crying? Sarah thought she could hear her turn away from the phone. She imagined the smooth contours of Julie's narrow face contorted for Julie, like her mother, did not cry easily.

"Sweetheart, what is it?"

"Wait," Julie begged, at which point she began to sob unmistakably, so there could be no doubt.

"All right. Take your time," Sarah said, her heart pounding, imagining the worst while trying to sound calm, silently planning a cross-country rescue.

Sarah climbed out of the bath and again wrapped the towel around her. She leaned on the sink for balance. A minute went by. Sarah clutched the phone. She collected her thoughts. The digital clock on the bathroom radio changed times from 10:19 to 10:20. 1:20 a.m. in New York—late but not unusually late for someone Julie's age. Maybe she'd had an argument with one of her room-mates. Or something had happened with the play. Maybe, after all, it was nothing irreparable. Sarah waited for Julie's breathing to become more regular. She wondered what her daughter was wearing, if she was cold, if she was alone in the dark.

"Julie, you have to try and tell me what's going on."

Sarah imagined Julie sitting on her bed in a small bedroom strewn with clothes, books, and papers—sheet music, pages of dialogue. When Julie cried, if she cried long enough, the pale skin on her face became blotchy with reddish, raised patches as though bees had stung her.

"Julie?"

"What?"

"Talk to me. Please."

"I will, but not over the phone," Julie said. Sarah thought she heard the snap of a lighter and her daughter inhale smoke.

"Are you smoking, Julie? I thought you'd quit!"

"Mom, please don't lecture me now," she exhaled loudly. "Anyway, the occasion seemed to call for it."

Sarah loosened her grasp on the phone and stood up, stretching her neck to either side. She began to pace. She walked into her bedroom glancing at the clock as she did so. "Julie it's very late. Maybe we should talk tomorrow."

"Maybe."

"Well?" Sarah knew she sounded impatient and regretted it.

"I was raped." Julie said.

Sarah stood still. "What?"

Julie did not answer.

"Did you say you were raped?" Sarah asked this question quietly and clearly.

"I don't even know his name," Julie whispered, her voice trembling, as though she had been heaved into the frozen New York night without her coat.

Sarah felt as though she had entered a strange, new universe. "Julie, you must go to a hospital; I believe the hospital will call the police. I'll catch a plane to New York in the morning, although I won't be there until late," she calculated the hours in transit, the time difference, "but I'll get there as soon as I can. Julie, are you listening to me?" Sarah stepped from the bedroom hallway into the living room and looked at the boxes and books on the floor, the piles of things to be given away.

"No, Mom," Julie said.

Sarah looked through the glass doors along the back of the house, black except for her own reflection.

"No, *what*? Julie?"

"I'm not sure I *want* you to come here. *I* don't want to be here. Do you understand? I don't want you to come to New York—I want to go *home*."

In one instant everything had changed. Sarah's heart broke for Julie but she needed to be stronger than her daughter. She would have to convince Julie to listen to her, to see—and this she would have to communicate gently—where Julie's own judgment had failed her.

"Sweetie, I don't think you're in a position to decide what's best for you." And as soon as the words left Sarah's mouth and were irretrievably transformed into electronic impulses, she knew she had said the wrong thing.

Julie ended the call. She called again but Julie let it go to voice mail. Sarah could almost see the tears fall from Julie's dark brown eyes and down her cheeks. Sarah pushed the redial button and the phone rang again and again without Julie answering.

The next time Sarah called she left a message. "I'm sorry for what I said. I didn't mean to be harsh. I love you, Julie. You know that. Call me, sweetheart. We'll figure out what to do—together." Sarah hung up and stood by the phone for a minute, contemplating what she should do next. I'm not the enemy, thought Sarah, just the closest target.

David. Why wasn't David here to fix this? She hadn't felt this helpless since the early weeks after the funeral. Julie wanted to come home but they didn't *have* a home anymore! Maybe, Sarah thought wildly, she should try and get out of the deal. But that was crazy. The house was sold; she had to finish packing. She had 45 days before escrow closed. She hadn't decided, at least not conclusively, where she would go. It had all happened so fast. Other than asking for the leave from work she didn't really have a plan. There had been no time to conceive of one. She could call her sister, Becca—what time was it in Chicago? No, too late and anyhow what could Becca do? Or say? She would undoubtedly imply, subtly of course, that it was Sarah's fault. How *had* this happened? Hadn't she cautioned Julie before she went to New York—and after? Sarah couldn't remember. Sarah knew she was going in circles. She pulled on a robe and went back in the bathroom. She took out the cosmetic bag she used for traveling. She opened a drawer and reached for her tweezers, q-tips, toothbrush, and travel-size plastic jars. But she left them on the counter in disarray and walked toward the kitchen. Coffee. She would make coffee and phone the airlines to see about morning flights. Then she walked back through the living room and pulled her suitcase out of the hall closet. She began to fill it with sweaters. She would need other things but just then she couldn't think of what and sweaters were warm and New York.... She envisioned a cold, black yawning city. She returned to the bathroom and stared at the collection of jars and tubes on the ceramic tile counter. Nothing made sense. If only Julie would call back.

# 7

Sarah walked to her gate and called the office. Tania answered the phone.

"Good morning, Tania. Is Maddy in?" asked Sarah. Maddy was the Director of the Annual Fund as well as the office manager.

"She's in a meeting. Where are you?"

Ignoring the question, she asked, "What about Parker?"

"Just a minute," Tania said and put Sarah on hold.

"Sarah?" Peggy Parker had worked for Sarah doing their gift processing for the past year. She was going to school at night to get her teaching credential, trying to put her life back together after a crummy divorce—no kids. She was thirty-five, plain, overweight, reliable and smart. She preferred to be called by her last name; hated the name she'd been given.

"I'm at the airport in Burbank. Julie's in trouble and I'm on my way to New York. I know the timing is awful," said Sarah, glad she'd gotten Parker on the line.

"Family comes first," said Parker.

"Tell that to John Carver—no don't," said Sarah. She realized she had not yet told her staff about the summer leave.

Parker laughed. "Yeah," she said. Then she added, "Is it bad?"

"I think so," said Sarah.

"Take it easy, then. Things are under control here. The responses for the Alumni Dinner are coming in. A few of the big shots have RSVP'd. Try not to stress."

"You're the best, Parker."

"Fly safe," she said.

ॐॐ

Sarah pushed the button for Julie's unit.

"Yeah?" It was Julie's voice.

"It's Mom," Sarah said.

Sarah had waited to call Julie until she was on the plane just before they were asked to turn off their phones. It was too late, she had told Julie over her objections, to change plans now.

"I'm coming up," Sarah said, trying to sound authoritative but loving. "We'll go to dinner."

Sarah rode the small elevator to Julie's third floor flat. Julie stood in the hall, her arms folded across her chest and for a minute Sarah thought of Claire, beaming, waiting for her. It was a good thing Claire would never know about this.

Julie walked up to Sarah and Sarah dropped the handle of her suitcase and reached for her daughter. Julie began to cry and Sarah held her close, both women tall, nearly the same height. It wasn't until they drew apart that Sarah considered Julie's face.

Her pallor could be attributed to a long Northeast winter but what Sarah detected went deeper than that. It was as if the life-blood had been drawn from the girl. Except for the red blotches that were beginning to show on her skin she could have been rendered in black and white. She was dressed in an oversized gray sweatshirt and jeans. It physically hurt Sarah but it was better to see Julie this way, better she not try to hide her misery. For, actress that she was, she could have pulled that off if she had wanted to, if she had been afraid to let Sarah in.

A bedroom door opened and another girl walked out. "It's so great that you're here," she said, running her hand through a short, curly mop of blond hair. "I'm Amelia, Julie's room mate." She was also young, also dressed in a sweatshirt and jeans but the difference between Julie and Amelia was palpable. Amelia fairly brimmed with energy.

"Danny and I—Danielle, that's our other room-mate, really wanted to help. You know, go to the police. Hang this creep up by his balls but Julie didn't want us to get *involved*."

Julie interrupted her. "It wasn't that. I understood what you guys wanted to do. I just didn't think it would change anything."

"See," said Amelia as if something had been proven. "I interned at the D.A.'s office last summer. It's amazing how few rapes get reported. Either the victim feels ashamed—you know—humiliated or else she just thinks no one will do anything and she'll have to spend all this time and it will all be a waste."

Julie, stricken, looked first at her mother then Amelia. "We're going to dinner," she said.

"Oh, OK," said Amelia. "I didn't mean to barge in–"

"You are very kind, Amelia," Sarah said. "Maybe we can talk later. I'd like to spend some time with Julie right now. We—we haven't seen each other...", Sarah's voice trailed off.

Amelia nodded and returned to her room, quietly closing the door.

"Amelia's parents are divorced," Julie said.

"I think we may have hurt her feelings."

"Uh,uh," said Julie, shaking her head in disagreement, her dark hair hanging limp against the sides of her face, her eyes rimmed in bluish circles. "She's tough. This never would have happened to her."

The New York night was neither empty nor black but bright and full of motion. It was windy and the wind made the air feel colder than it was and even Julie's heavy woolen coat could not keep her from shivering. Sarah imagined Julie wearing the coat on the way home from his apartment. Last night. Could it have happened just the night before? Couldn't they simply undo the previous 24 hours? She tried not to think about it, tried to keep the pictures out of her head but it wasn't much use. The two women walked the four blocks to the restaurant in silence, arm in arm.

Once seated at Nino's, a small neighborhood Italian, a waiter appeared at their table and asked about drinks. Sarah pointed to a half-bottle of Chianti on the menu and he brought it to them with a basket of bread. After some of each Julie finally removed her coat.

"That sweater looks nice on you," said Sarah. Julie was wearing the pale yellow sweater Sarah had sent for her birthday in September. It had always been easy to buy Julie gifts. A thin slice of pain crossed Sarah's heart as she recalled September, other birthdays, any time before.

"You bought it for me," said Julie, drinking the wine.

"Yes, I remember."

There was an awkward moment after which Sarah tried again to begin a conversation.

"Have you spoken with the director of the play?"

"About what?"

"I don't know. Returning to work?" Sarah dipped a piece of bread in olive oil.

"We're dark tonight and tomorrow night."

"I meant are you going to stay in New York? You said something about coming home."

Julie looked at Sarah. She didn't seem to have an answer. Sarah paused, then went on. "I've asked my realtor for an extension of the escrow period."

"What's that?"

"It's the time between selling the house and moving out. If I'd known...," Sarah cast about for the right words. "I mean your room is half packed."

Julie sat up with an alarmed look on her face. "You went through my stuff?"

"I had to start putting everything in boxes. I haven't thrown anything out. Really I haven't. Except maybe some socks with holes and old underwear. Magazines—things like that. No books or records or—"

"You went through my *underwear?*" Julie's eyebrows arched, and color now flushed her face.

"Oh, Julie. I wasn't looking for anything! And someone had to do it! You've been away—"

"I came back when Daddy was sick," Julie said.

"Yes, you did."

Julie looked like she was about to cry again. "I may have left something *important* in my room!"

"Don't worry, honey. Please don't."

"I wish Daddy was here now," Julie said, her voice wavering, musical. "He used to tell me I had a sweet life."

"You do, Julie. Oh, you *do.*"

The tears began to run down Julie's cheeks and she wiped them away with the back of her hand. Sarah pulled some Kleenex out of her purse and reached across the table holding it out to Julie but Julie had her head in her hands and was crying hard without making a sound. Sarah laid the Kleenex by her plate.

# 8

In the end, Julie flew back to L.A. with Sarah. Julie's roommates begged Julie to report the rape to the District Attorney. Sarah urged Julie to go to Columbia Presbyterian to be checked out. But Julie refused; she wanted to get out of New York as soon as possible. She called the director at home and told him she had go back to L.A. He told her that the part might not be there for her when she returned. He didn't know how long a run they would have. She told him she was aware of the consequences of her action but there was a family emergency that required her presence. She didn't elaborate. Sarah sat in the apartment and listened while Julie made the call. When Julie got off the phone she told Sarah she didn't think she would be coming back to New York anyway.

Rain pummeled the wings of the plane as it taxied out. The takeoff was bumpy and Julie's hands were white from her tight grip on the armrests. Sarah put her hand on Julie's arm while Julie stared out of the window.

Once the plane had leveled off, the flight attendant made it down the aisle to their seat. Sarah asked Julie if she wanted anything.

"A Bloody Mary, please," Julie said.

"I'll have one too," Sarah added.

"Do you want to watch the movie?" asked Sarah, still not sure when the right time would be to talk about everything.

"I guess," said Julie. "What is it?"

"I'm not sure," said Sarah who had already taken out the file folder she had brought with her. It was the first time she had opened it since arriving in New York.

"Ugh," said Julie. "It's some action movie."

"Why don't you close your eyes?" said Sarah. "Even if you don't sleep you can rest."

"Sometimes you're such a *Mom*," said Julie, the ends of her mouth turning up slightly—the hint of a smile. With her eyes closed, her dark lashes—David's thick lashes—almost touched her cheek. Sarah pushed a lock of hair away from Julie's face with her hand and, without opening her eyes Julie held Sarah's hand to her forehead. It was something Julie used to do when she was little and it took Sarah back in time. She would try to get her energetic child to nap by stroking her head. Julie would clasp Sarah's hand to her cheek or forehead. "Mommy don't go", she would say. Sarah's heart was full, remembering in a rush the moments of Julie's life.

On the way to Woodland Hills Sarah phoned Jean Bartlett.

"Jean. Hi it's Sarah. I thought I would've heard from you," said Sarah.

"I know, I know," Jean said, sounding hassled, the flutter of paper in the background. "I've been trying to get the month you need but the buyers can only manage another two weeks. Does that help? It's the best I can do."

"It will," she said, half responding to Jean, half thinking out loud. "I should know where things stand pretty soon."

The cab driver, who had been carrying on his own cell phone conversation in a language Sarah didn't recognize, leaned on his horn as a truck cut in front of him.

"Where *are* you?" Jean asked.

Sarah turned to look at Julie, the white-coated wires of her iPod trailing down from her ears. "We're on our way home," she said.

When Sarah got back to the office the next day there was a stack of messages in her mail slot. Tania sauntered in to inform her of what she had missed and what was on the calendar.

"The Dean wants you to call him as soon as you get in," Tania said, studying a list she had written out in her lovely penmanship. The graceful hand and the bad attitude didn't go together.

"OK. What else?" Sarah asked, thumbing through the messages as she listened, noting that there were two from Dean Carver in her stack and one from a V.P. for Development she had met in San Diego.

"The Board meeting is at 3 this afternoon," Tania peered at Sarah with disapproval.

"Why didn't someone leave a message reminding me about the Board meeting?" Sarah asked. "I would have worn a suit and heels."

"We assumed you knew," said Tania.

"Someone *did* notify the dean that I had to go to New York for a family emergency. Didn't they?" Sarah fumed.

"Don't ask *me*," said Tania.

Sarah disliked Tania and looked forward to getting rid of her but she needed to do a performance evaluation and she hadn't had the time. Besides, she hated confrontations with staff.

When Sarah got home later that evening she found Julie lying on the couch in the family room watching a black-and-white movie on TV and eating a slice of pizza off a paper plate. Sarah sat down next to Julie, propping Julie's feet on her lap.

"What's on?" Sarah asked, trying to keep her tone light. Julie was still in her sweats, hair uncombed, fuzzy slippers under the coffee table. It was clear she had not showered or left the house all day.

"A movie," Julie mumbled, pizza in her mouth.

"Casablanca!" said Sarah.

"Yeah," said Julie. Sarah became absorbed in the film. She dropped her purse and briefcase to the floor and eventually kicked off her shoes, which landed next to Julie's slippers under the coffee table.

# 9

The Valley Sexual Assault and Recovery Center was located in a small suite of offices on the second floor of an office building in a transitional part of town. One block housed the Van Nuys City Hall and the Los Angeles County Superior Court for the Northwest District. Manicured lawns and cement walkways separated the government buildings from the rest of Van Nuys Boulevard which was lined to the north and south with storefronts. Spanish language banners floated above them; the shops themselves were crammed full of blouses, pants and jackets hanging from the rafters and in colorful rows along the walls.

Julie had been back in L.A. for over a week when Sarah decided it was time for them to deal with what had happened in New York. They hadn't talked about it. Sarah had treated Julie as though she had been sick, letting her lounge around the house while Sarah went to work. Sarah would call Julie during the day, waking her often at noon, or later, and discuss nothing more complicated than what they would do for dinner that night. But Sarah felt their denial could not go on any longer; they had to figure out what to do. Sarah researched some counseling options and learned about the Center through Valley Family Services—a non-profit organization she and David had supported in the past.

Tammy Fuentes met Sarah and Julie in the waiting area at two sharp. Tammy was around 40 and wore her light brown, curly hair loosely tied back, escaped wisps of it framing her pretty face.

J.S. Tyndall

"Would you like some tea?" Tammy offered as she motioned for Sarah and Julie to take their seats.

They shook their heads. Tammy nodded. She shut the door and sat down behind her desk. A moment elapsed before Tammy spoke again. "Julie, your mother called us to make this appointment. How do you feel about that?"

"I don't know," said Julie.

Tammy looked steadily at Julie. "Let me tell you what we do here. We're a place where people can come to talk about how they were sexually assaulted or abused. Everything that goes on here is confidential. Unlike hospitals, we are not required to report anything to the police unless the victim wants us to."

"I hate that word—victim," said Julie, her head down.

"We're going to get to that," Tammy said softly. "Did you know that, officially only 16 per cent of rapes are reported?"

"My room mate worked in the D.A.'s office in New York. I know all about it."

"But that doesn't mean a lot of women don't get help in other ways."

Julie looked bored, adolescent. Coming to the Center was her mother's idea. "I really don't want to think about this," she said.

"I know. It's hard." She paused and looked at Julie. "Do you plan to stay in New York?"

"Why?"

"I'm just trying to get a feel for how long you'll be here. The weeks and months after a rape—"

"I don't know if I was—technically—raped."

"OK," Tammy said. "Julie, I think we need to talk about some specifics. Would you like your mother to stay with us? I'm sure she'd be OK to wait outside." Tammy looked from Julie to

Sarah. Sarah held her breath, not sure what she wanted Julie to say.

"She can stay," Julie said.

Sarah's stomach twisted into a tight knot. She forced a smile and moved her chair a bit closer to Julie's. She hadn't wanted to push. She hadn't wanted to know.

"All right then. Can you tell us what happened?" Tammy asked, using a gentle but firm voice.

Julie stared out of the window, looking at neither woman. "I was forced to have oral sex with someone—a stranger."

Tammy continued in a smooth tone without surprise or emotion in it. "Julie, forced oral sex is considered felony rape. Period. It is no less a crime—and no less traumatic—than rape through intercourse."

Julie sat quietly. She focused on the wisps of hair around Tammy's face, the laugh lines around her clear brown eyes. She was listening now.

"Really?" asked Julie.

Tammy nodded and went on. "There are some things I would like to ask you, regardless of whether or not you decide to pursue any legal action. All right?" Julie nodded. "Did you keep any of the clothes you were wearing—I mean not launder them?"

"I took my clothes to the cleaners."

"Too bad. Sometimes the perpetrator leaves DNA on the victim's clothes and we can use that to identify him. But that's OK. I wanted to ask you if he had a weapon of any kind, if he threatened to harm you if you didn't do what he wanted?"

"He had a gun." Julie glanced at Sarah whose face turned ashen. "He didn't use it but it was there, on top of the TV."

"The threat was implied then," Tammy jotted notes on a legal pad. She looked up at Julie. "If you do decide to stay in the area we have a fine program here at the Center. Our counselors are great."

Both Tammy and Sarah watched Julie for her reaction but there was none. Her expression was blank.

Tammy leaned in toward Julie. "Let us try and help you through this process. It won't be easy but it's worth it. Every day we help young women like you reclaim their lives."

"I'm impressed with how you handled things today," Sarah said, once they were back in the car. Julie frowned and turned the radio on to a station she liked, ending the discussion before it began.

As they neared the house, Sarah slowed the car down on Ventura Boulevard. "Would you like to get some coffee?" she asked.

"He said he had a *club* - " Julie's words came in a rush and her voice rose. *"He wanted to hear me sing!"*

"It's all right," Sarah said, and drove on. "I understand."

Sarah had forgotten that she made plans to go out with a friend that evening. She called to cancel.

"I'm sorry I didn't call sooner but I need to spend time with Julie," she said, without explanation. Julie had gone into her room and closed the door. Sarah could hear music playing. She was about to knock but withdrew her hand, standing at the door to Julie's room. She was glad that her daughter was safe inside. It was almost as though she had never left.

Sarah decided to make it a Saturday night at home. She ordered Chinese—something she and David used to do on weekends when they didn't have plans or feel like going out. They would eat dinner off the coffee table in the family room and watch a movie.

"New York has amazing Chinese food," Julie said, displaying an appetite that pleased Sarah.

"I'll bet," said Sarah.

"I don't want to live there anymore, you know."

Sarah was not prepared for that remark. Raising her eyebrows, she asked, "What about the apartment?".

"They'll be able to find someone to replace me in a heartbeat. You saw it. It's in a great location, close to everything. Amelia's father owns the apartment anyway. All I have to do is send for my stuff."

"Well," Sarah hesitated, "what about your job?"

"There's a lot going on outside of New York," Julie responded. "Anyway, I'm not sure I still want to perform."

"Really? Why, do you think?"

"Daddy always believed I had talent. I don't know—that's not even it. It's being *up* there—on stage. I'm not the girl Dad wanted me to be—'try out for this, audition for that'. But I knew he'd be disappointed if I didn't make the effort."

Sarah put down her chopsticks, listening.

Julie went on. "I don't think it was a waste—to major in drama, go to New York and all. I met some amazing people. And," she said solemnly, "I learned a lot."

"I'm sure that's true," said Sarah.

"I mean in a *good* way. Anyhow, can we start the movie now?" asked Julie. Her plate was half-full and take-out boxes covered the table.

"Sure. Why not?" Sarah said, trying to sound upbeat, realizing how young Julie was.

# 10

The following week, Sarah received an e-mail from written in halting English from M. Vannerie, the owner of an apartment in Paris.

Sarah stared at the screen. She had forgotten about the note she had written inquiring about the apartment. She had just come home from work and she and Julie were planning to go out to get something to eat.

They drove to Saul's Deli. Sarah and David had gone to Saul's often in the weeks and months after he was diagnosed. They would order matzoh ball soup and talk. Saul's was a place for talks. The booths were oversized and comfortable and the waitresses kept filling up your coffee mug for as long as you wanted to stay. After David died, Sarah continued to go there once a week, usually on Thursdays. She would order soup and a beer and a half corned beef sandwich. The waitresses would tell her about their own troubles. It was the only place where she didn't feel strange eating alone.

Tonight, Donna was their waitress. Donna had two kids from her first husband and one from the second. Neither father stayed around to help raise the kids, leaving her twice a single mom.

"Evening Sarah," Donna said. "Julie."

"Want to share a corned beef sandwich with me?" Sarah asked Julie.

"I don't know. I'll just have some soup,"

"Matzoh ball?" asked Donna, writing on her pad.

"Sure," said Julie. "Thanks—oh, and a Diet Coke."

"I'll have my regular," said Sarah.

"That'll be two matzoh balls, a half corned beef on rye, a Diet and a light beer." Donna tore the top page off, stuck the pad back in her pocket and said she'd be right back with their drinks.

Sarah tried to think of the best way to bring up the idea of going to France. She didn't know herself whether it made sense anymore. She and Julie had not discussed much past the move out of the house.

"I got an e-mail today from a man who owns an apartment in Paris," Sarah began. "He's a friend of a friend of Daddy's."

"And?" Julie asked, sipping her Diet Coke.

"Well, he was answering a note I'd sent him about renting his apartment for a month this summer. It was before I learned about what happened to you in New York."

"So you're going to Europe this summer?"

"I don't know—I have thought about it. I've already asked my boss, the dean, for a leave. You know I've been at Kelton Hall a long time and—"

"That sounds cool. You should go." Julie sounded almost casual, flip. "You had said something about renting an apartment at Oakhurst. I could stay there. They have a pool. Jessica's parents stayed there when they were redoing their house. And, I could use your car, right?"

"You see," Sarah hesitated, "I can't afford to do both—keep an apartment at Oakhurst and rent a place in France. Originally, I'd thought I would sell our house and move into a new place. But the house sold quicker than I'd expected and I decided to take this leave and you came home and—"

"And what? I spoiled your plans? Gee, I'm sorry I was raped. It's so messy..." Her voice rose.

"Shhh," Sarah said. "No, the thing is I'd like you to come with me."

"To Paris?" Julie tilted her head and raised her eyebrows. Her cheeks were pink with emotion.

"Yes. And there's something else. I thought of spending the second month in the south of France. Maybe take a cooking class. I've always wanted to study cooking in a serious way."

"I've never been to Paris," Julie said.

"I know," smiled Sarah. "I think it would be good for you."

"*Good* for me? Like *therapy*? Like I'm some kind of damaged, *broken* thing?" Julie pushed the soup bowl away, crumpled her napkin and dropped it on the table.

"Is everything OK here?" Donna asked, appearing beside them.

"Fine," Sarah said.

Donna gave Sarah a sympathetic look and backed away, tearing off the check and leaving it on the table. "No rush," she said.

"Listen, sweetheart, here's what I think. I think you should come with me. I think we'll have a nice time and yes—it would be good for *both* of us to have some fun. But, you have options. You could stay here at Grandma's apartment and use my car while I'm away to go to the Center or get a part time job. Or, you could visit Aunt Becca and Uncle Mark. I don't know if Amy will be home during the summer but I bet you could spend time with her too. Or—and we need to discuss this because I need to let M. Vannerie know one way or the other—I could cancel my trip. We could keep the place at Oakhurst for the whole summer and take our time deciding what to do next."

Julie sat quietly across from Sarah tearing bits off the napkin.

"Julie?"

"What?" Julie replied—loud enough so other diners looked their way.

"Please..."

"What do you want, Mom. You want me to decide this minute?"

"No," Sarah sighed, "of course not."

Julie's lower lip trembled and she looked away from Sarah.

"This shouldn't be your problem," said Sarah.

"But it seems like it's all my problem—that I *am* the problem!" She muttered to herself it seemed, "Just getting in your way."

"Let's give it a rest for now," Sarah said. She picked up the check Donna had left on the table.

"Whatever," said Julie.

Sarah wrote to M. Vannerie and explained—without details—that unfortunately, things were up in the air. Sarah told him her daughter Julie might be accompanying her to Paris but if not, unless she could make satisfactory arrangements for Julie, Sarah might need to remain in Los Angeles. Thus, she could not commit absolutely. Could he, Sarah wrote in French later that night at her computer, consulting her dictionary often, possibly wait a little longer? He wrote back the next day that he fully understood how children complicated matters—he had two of his own. Was it enough for him to know that she *wanted* the apartment, Sarah asked in her next note. That if she could possibly manage it, she would take the apartment for the month? She was willing to send him a deposit. M. Vannerie told Sarah to let him know her intentions as soon as she could and the deposit wasn't necessary until she confirmed.

Over the next two weeks Julie and Sarah went back and forth about the trip. Julie would come with her to Paris but not Provence. Julie wouldn't go at all but would visit her Aunt in Chicago. It was where she had gone to school; she had been happy there. She had friends in Chicago. It was not New York but it was like New York with a lively theater scene. Or Sarah could forget the whole thing.

In the end Julie chose what Sarah considered to be the least likely arrangement. Julie decided to stay at Claire's apartment with Asya and Claire. She would sleep in the den on the fold-out bed. Tammy and the others at the Valley Sexual Assault and Recovery Center had encouraged her to stay in L.A. They referred her to the Santa Monica Rape Crisis Center and told her who to speak to there. They even arranged to have her talk with the volunteer coordinator in Santa Monica to see about working there a few hours a week. They believed it was important for Julie to work through her anger.

Sarah discussed the idea with Asya on the phone one evening after the Julie had not wavered for a full twenty-four hours.

"Julie she is fine with us. Good for her to spend time with her grandmother," said Asya. "Sarah, you work so hard, you have not had easy time. Paris! Ah, this I love. You should go while you are still young."

"I hope she won't be too much extra work for you," Sarah said.

"No. She's good girl. She will help me!" said Asya with apparent confidence.

Sarah wasn't so sure.

"In any case, I won't be leaving for another ten days. I still have to move out of our house."

"Ah," said Asya. Sarah could imagine her shaking her head. "You have so much to do. But we will be fine. We have friends in the building. Claire's doctors—they all know me. And I cook for Julie. I make moussaka! She will like."

# 11

The morning they were to move, the sky was pale and spattered with rose-gold clouds preceding the sun. Julie was still asleep. Sarah would wake her shortly but for now she wanted the house to herself, her home of fifteen years, the one she and David had shared, the one she was about to leave forever.

Wearing an old T-shirt of David's, Sarah padded into the kitchen to put on the coffee—the movers said she could leave one kitchen box unsealed until they arrived—and stood at the sink waiting for it to brew. Her Persian neighbor across the street was leaning against his old white Toyota, smoking a cigarette before getting into the car to go to work. Her thoughts flew out to him: Good-bye!

Jean Bartlett had suggested leaving a bottle of Champagne for the new owners, the young couple. When Sarah opened the refrigerator to get the milk for coffee she saw the bottle of Veuve Cliquot she had purchased for them. Propped against the bottle was a note which she had written. She wanted to read it one more time but it was sealed tight. Wanting to open that note felt like everything else—that things were proceeding irrevocably, that there was no turning back. She tried to remember what she had written. Something about having been happy there.

Sarah took the milk out of the refrigerator and closed the door. The sky was already brighter. The sun had risen above the trees and houses to the east. She opened Julie's door to wake her.

Julie groaned and said, "I'm up."

"The movers will be here soon," said Sarah, heading for the bathroom with her coffee.

Just as she turned off the blow dryer, Sarah heard the rumble of a truck. It was time to go.

֍

The one-bedroom apartment at Oakhurst that was to be home for the next two weeks was beige—almost all beige with some pastel hues scattered about on pillows and bedspreads. The kitchen was well equipped, Sarah thought, as she inventoried the pots and pans and cooking utensils. Julie was in her bedroom. They had sent for a box of her things from the apartment in New York and she was going through them for the first time. Sarah called to her.

"Julie?"

"What?"

"How does Chicken Piccata sound for dinner tonight?"

Julie walked out of her bedroom. She was wearing a pair of short, cut-off jeans and a tank top.

"With lots of pasta?" Julie asked

"Yep. Lots."

"But I'm dieting…"

"That's absurd. You're getting too thin. And, it's one of your favorites. So will you go to the store for me?"

Nodding, Julie said, "I was going out anyway."

"My keys are on the counter," Sarah pointed. "When will you be back? By six, OK?"

She watched her daughter and thought how far she had come since they had flown back from New York. Julie seemed stronger and more confident—more like her old self. Sarah wanted to believe that somehow she was lending Julie a portion of the strength she needed to continue to heal. As they spent more time together, Julie seemed to have grown used to the idea of Sarah leaving for France. She had agreed to consider joining her, perhaps for the last week of her stay in Paris, or later in Provence, if that part came to pass.

Sarah gave Julie a shopping list that included chicken breasts, and asparagus.

"Look at the price before buying it. And, the tips should be closed. Frozen petite peas would be a good alternative," Sarah said.

Julie shook her head. "You are *so* picky!" She said as she grabbed the car keys and swung her backpack over her shoulder.

Sarah sat down on one of the stools that pulled up to the plain white tiled counter top that separated the kitchen from the living area. Sarah ran her hand over the tiles and recalled the hand-made cream-and-celadon colored tiles in her kitchen in Woodland Hills, the kitchen she had designed herself. She experienced such a mix of feelings. She missed *her* kitchen, her house, but at the same time she felt curiously unburdened.

The cell phone rang and for a minute she couldn't remember where it was. She thought she heard the tone coming from her purse but then remembered it was in its charger.

"Hello?"

"Sarah?" It was Jean Bartlett. "The funds are in. We had them wired to the account number you gave us. You can call your broker to make sure."

Sarah's chest tightened. "Thank you for everything, Jean."

"My pleasure. Now we have to find you another little nest of your own," Jean said cheerily.

Before Sarah could explain once again that she wasn't ready for another nest, Jean told her she had a call coming in that she had to take but that she would be in touch. And then she was gone. Sarah carefully placed the phone on the kitchen counter as though the phone itself was her connection to everything she had left behind.

It was done—over. Sarah was heady with the fact that $305,000 had just been deposited in her Fidelity brokerage account. Her liquid assets had more than tripled in the past few hours. She walked across the living room to the sliding glass door, turned the safety latch and jerked the door open, noticing the torn screen, testing the air. It was hot and dry and smelled of chlorine. The apartments were built in a hollow square with a swimming pool in the middle. Two teenaged girls in bikinis worked on their tans. Across the way, a woman with a boy at her feet hung some clothes to dry over the white plastic chairs on her patio. Sarah watched the woman scoop up the child and carry him back inside their unit.

Everything about the Oakhurst apartments was foreign and anonymous; in here she felt like a stranger even though she was less than two miles from the house in Woodland Hills. *David*, she spoke silently, *I did it!* Suddenly the emotions that had accumulated over the past days and weeks overwhelmed her. She pulled the sliding door closed, sank into a nearby chair and wept.

# 12

Sarah's desk was cleared of papers and her inbox was empty. She checked the clock—6:25 P.M. The meeting with Dean Carver was supposed to have been at six. She was tired and hungry and knew the traffic would be horrendous at this hour on a Friday. John Carver always kept her waiting. Not that she was alone. He treated all of his senior staff the same way. Not faculty, and certainly not alumni, but staff? It was one long loyalty test.

Sarah called upstairs. Chang answered with more than her usual weariness. "He's still meeting with the Advisory Committee. They were supposed to have been finished at 6. What do you want me to do?"

Sarah thought for a moment. "Tell him to have a good summer," she said.

Chang chuckled. "You really want me to say that?" She asked.

"No. You know what? I'll write a note and bring it up."

Sarah took out a Kelton Hall note pad and jotted a few words to the dean, thanking him for giving her this time off. She wrote down a contact number at Claire's in case there was some reason why he might need to get in touch with her. Her mother's caregiver would know how to reach her, she wrote.

Sarah gathered her things, took one long deep breath and turned off the computer and the lights in her office. She walked up the two flights of stairs and knocked on the locked door. Chang answered it with the wry smile she was famous for and let Sarah inside. Chang showed no signs of going home. Her desk was littered with papers and a document was pulled up on her computer screen. A Coke cup with melted ice sat in a small puddle of water beside her phone.

Sarah handed the note to Chang and was leaning down to give her a hug when the door to John Carver's office opened with the sound of voices.

"Hi, Sarah," said Andrea James, one of Sarah's favorite professors and a beloved teacher for over two decades of law students. "I hear you're escaping for a couple of months. Good for you!"

"I'll be back in the fall," said Sarah.

"She'd better," said John Carver who directed Sarah into his office with a nod. Sarah looked at Chang, her note still in Chang's hand. Chang shrugged her shoulders.

"You still here Chang?" Carver said. "Why don't you call it a day? Print out what you've got and I'll take it home with me this weekend—unless you'd like to come in and work with me on it tomorrow? We could make some decent headway without the phones ringing off the hook."

Sarah smiled at Chang in sympathy before walking into the dean's office.

Sarah and Julie spent the weekend packing up the Oakhurst apartment, separating things into piles. On Monday, they drove to Northridge and dropped off the box filled with clothes and other items she would add to her storage locker. Her suitcase for the trip and Julie's duffle and box of things from her New York apartment stayed in the car. As Sarah turned the Honda toward the San Diego freeway and Claire's apartment she developed a bad case of butterflies.

Julie played the radio too loud, but Sarah didn't ask her to lower the volume nor did she push any kind of conversation.

Asya and Claire greeted them at the door to the apartment. Claire looked puzzled as her daughter, grand-daughter and the doorman marched into the apartment with three pieces of luggage and Julie's large taped-up box.

Claire pointed to the entry hall and began speaking frantically and incomprehensibly to Sarah.

"It's OK," Sarah said, leading Claire into the living room.

"Mom," she began, "Julie is coming to stay here for a while. She wants to spend time with you."

"I *know*," said Claire, disarmingly coherent. Claire's gaze tracked the route into the den where Julie was already emptying her backpack. Claire nodded her head in Julie's direction and, begging comprehension, said in a loud voice, "What?"

Sarah again tried to explain, pulling Claire down on the sofa and taking her hand but Claire withdrew it in a fit of frustration.

"I'm going to France for a bit," Sarah said, losing her nerve, her voice shaky. "I may stay longer if it works out and Julie may come over to visit me later in the summer. I will call you once a week and Asya will have my number in Paris. Do you understand? I don't want you to worry."

Claire made a fist and shook it at Sarah. Sarah's left eye began to twitch, something that occurred when she was stressed to her limit. Claire got up and at first Sarah thought her mother might try and strike her but instead Claire walked into the entry way and pointed angrily to the suitcases. Then she looked at Sarah for an answer.

Sarah had forgotten that her mother no longer had the capacity to think in abstract terms. The confusion in her mother's brain required as much order and routine as possible to counter the inner chaos.

Asya quickly joined Claire in the hall. "These?" Asya asked. "You want we move these?"

Claire breathed a huge sigh and unclenched her fists, smiling at Asya.

Sarah walked over to her mother and in a gentle voice said, "I'll be taking those suitcases with me in a few hours, when Julie takes me to the airport. They'll be out of your way, I promise."

"Good," Claire said emphatically and went in to sit down at the dining room table.

"You see?" Asya said to Sarah with an expression that spoke volumes about the difficulties of taking care of Claire. She went into the kitchen and came out with a piece of chocolate, a glass of water and a half a banana, which she gave to Claire. Claire concentrated on the small feast in front of her, appearing to have put the previous scene entirely out of her mind.

Sarah stared at her mother, this woman whom she had known her entire life. The twitch in her eye muscle began to subside but the feelings of desperation that she had absorbed from the exchange did not.

By the time Sarah and Julie were to leave for the airport, Asya was busy preparing dinner. Tonight she would serve a roasted chicken, the kind one picked up fully cooked at the grocery store. Claire had gone in to her bedroom to watch television. Julie had stayed in the den, reading and making phone calls. Sarah had been on the phone as well with Becca confirming last minute arrangements.

"They all seem so vulnerable," Sarah said to Becca, Sarah's sister in Chicago, as they were concluding their conversation.

"They are," said Becca. "But you have to do what you have to do."

Sarah sighed deeply—guilt, obligation—it seemed endless.

"The Paris apartment is big enough for Julie to come and stay if it gets to be too much here. I wanted her to come with me, Becca. But she wouldn't!"

"I know all about it. You gave Julie a choice. You even offered to stay in L.A."

Sarah could tell Becca was not impressed.

"It could work," Sarah said, her voice sounding small.

"It could," said Becca.


Sarah drove the Honda to LAX with Julie beside her in the passenger seat.

"You have your license with you, right?" asked Sarah.

"God, Mom!"

"You might want to take Sepulveda back to Santa Monica this time of day. Do you know that route?"

"Mom, I'm gonna be OK."

Sarah, tried to remember the speech she had intended to make to Julie on the way to the airport but they were already at Manchester and Sarah couldn't think of how to start.

"Julie," Sarah cleared her voice. "The apartment, you know, in Paris—I told you there was room. I wish you were coming, sweetheart."

"No you don't, not really," said Julie in a matter of fact voice.

Sarah turned to look at her. "That's not true!"

"Think about it Mom. You're going to have an adventure. Forty and fabulous in Paris…"

"Hardly forty—"

"You know what I mean. Having your daughter there would cramp your style." Julie was trying to sound upbeat and glib but it wasn't working. The ends of her mouth began to tremble.

"Julie, I'm *terrified* of going to Paris alone."

"You are?"

Sarah nodded. "I'm pushing myself. You know about that kind of thing—like you've been doing since coming home. I don't want to become bitter. I've seen too many sad and bitter women who've lost their husbands to death or divorce. Ones who never recover...I *want* to recover. I want to be happy again—at least try -even if I am scared."

"Like me."

"Yes." None of this was what Sarah had planned to say but it was all right.

"Are you OK?" Sarah asked as she pulled off at the Century Blvd. Exit, and stopped at the signal. She leaned over the armrests and gave Julie an awkward hug.

"I'm fine," Julie said, holding tight to her mother while the car behind them honked as the light had changed to green.

# 13

The plane descended through a thin layer of clouds revealing first the Channel, then the beaches, the variously green quilt of fields and finally the sprawling, spectacular gray of the city, the Eiffel Tower rising in a lacey iron grid.

The sky was pale and overcast and the air smelled of exhaust. Taxis lined up waiting to transport arriving passengers into the city. Sarah Coleman made eye contact with the blonde driver of a silver-blue Mercedes, next in the queue.

She called to the driver and he jumped out, heaved her bags into the trunk and opened the door of the back seat, waiting politely until she was settled.

Sarah dug in her purse for the slip of paper. "17 Avenue Souffren," she said.

Sarah watched as he consulted his portable GPS.

Paris. She and David Sarah had wanted to return one day. Travel to the South, rent a house, cook and.... There were so many things they had wanted to do.

Recalling Paris with David, she pictured the tiny hotel room on the Avenue de l' Université where they made love in the late afternoon on the too soft bed. All those years ago, she had risen one night and stood in her thin nightgown by the window that opened onto a cul-de-sac and the granite clock tower of the Sorbonne. The face of the immense clock was lit by the moon. It was as perfectly rendered in her mind as if it were a photograph.

An abrupt stop of the taxi and the squeal of brakes startled her for she must have dozed off. When she looked through the window she could see the Arc de Triomphe in the distance.

"Oh, my God!"

"Sorry, Madame!"

"No—no, it's not that," Sarah said.

The driver nodded as though he understood, looking in his rear view mirror at the well-dressed, attractive woman in the back seat.

"Bienvenue à Paris," he said with a smile. Welcome to Paris.

He carried Sarah's luggage up the steps to 17 Avenue Soufren. "Bonjour?" a male voice answered when she rang apartment #26. He said he would be right down.

A young man with dark hair that fell in his eyes as he opened the heavy front door jogged towards her.

"Michel? Your parents told me you would be here."

"Oui, Madame Coleman, he answered pushing his hair back. We will go upstairs?"

"One minute," Sarah replied and turned to the driver.

"Merci, monsieur." Sarah felt grateful for his words, even more for his silence, and gave him a generous tip.

"Bonnes vacances, Madame!" He shouted as she followed Michel inside.

Michel and Sarah crowded into the tiny elevator with its accordion-style gate and rode it to the third floor.

Once inside the apartment, Sarah took stock of her surroundings. The owners, George and Catherine Vannerie, had retired from academic careers and liked to travel. Renting out their well-situated flat supplied them the means to do so on their modest pensions.

The living room and bedroom faced the street and had tall glass doors that opened onto a small balcony. From the kitchen window one could see the unmistakable white dome of Sacre Coeur far in the distance. Someone had stocked the refrigerator with milk, butter and a bottle of Rose. On the counter sat a bowl of fruit—bananas and strawberries—a package of coffee and a crisp, brown baguette wrapped in white paper. Sarah smiled.

"How thoughtful! Merci, Michel." Tall and thin, he reminded her of someone with his shock of dark hair. Sarah guessed him to be around thirty.

"It is nothing, Madame."

"I communicated with your father via e-mail in French but my French is only fair. I hope we understood each other!"

"Of course," he said, his hair falling again in his eyes, like Julie's did. That was it. He reminded her of Julie.

"Something is wrong, Madame?"

"I—I was just thinking of my daughter. How she would like it here."

"She has been to Paris?"

"No."

"A shame," he said. "Perhaps she comes to visit while you stay in Paris?" He pointed to the alcove off the living room which held a bed covered with a yellow quilt. He walked quickly to a linen closet in the hall and opened it. It contained blankets, sheets and sleeping pillows. He began to describe its contents when Sarah touched his arm.

"Michel, could we discuss the rental agreement? I'm really quite tired."

He shrugged. "Of course," he said, gesturing toward the dining table upon which lay a folder with papers. Sarah felt she had been abrupt and apologized. She offered to make some coffee.

"Merci, but no, Madame," Michel said. "In any case, I must go to work. I teach at the Sorbonne—L'Histoire."

"That's impressive," said Sarah.

"I am only assistant professeur, so I must be on time for my classes."

"Of course," said Sarah. "Now, let's see what we have." She sat down at the table.

"My parents will be gone for only one month. If you wish to stay in Paris longer, we will help you find something comparable.

"Actually, I was thinking of traveling on to Provence -"

"This is a coincidence, I think! Father's sister—my Aunt Pauline—lets her home in Provence from time to time. It is a simple mas—a small, old farmhouse—in Mausanne-les-Alpilles not far from St. Remy. We can speak to her if you wish."

"How kind. May I call you in a few days? I can't think clearly about much of anything right now. Do I have your phone number?"

Michel pointed to the packet. "It is all in there."

Sarah signed the rental agreement and handed Michel 2000 Euros for the month. It was a bargain for a such a well located apartment Sarah thought as she said good-bye, noticing the quiet once she closed the door, hearing only his footsteps in the hall and the whirring of the elevator mechanism, taking him down to the street.

Sarah busied herself with unpacking, not allowing the rising sense of panic to spoil the charm of the apartment and her first day in Paris. She had taken a chance, risked her job and defied her sense of duty and obligation to Julie and her mother Claire to do this thing. John Carver had granted her a leave of absence for the summer. That in itself was amazing. And it was difficult enough, traveling to Paris alone, but she had done it and she'd be damned if she was going to going to have a meltdown now.

Stepping on to the balcony Sarah leaned her arms on the railing; it was cold and wet. A plume of unease spread through her as she watched the clouds and the lights of the city obscure all but a few stars. The combined smells of diesel oil, geraniums and cigarette smoke were familiar, reminiscent. She returned to the room, leaving the window ajar.

The next morning she woke late. Before anything else she drew back the curtains to look out. The skies had cleared. The windows, open all night, let in the almost balmy air; it was a beautiful spring day. The street below was charmingly ordinary if anything in Paris could be called ordinary. Today it seemed that everyone was out—shopping, strolling and enjoying the city. Amidst the activity, Sarah felt keenly alone but more than that, she felt adrift, as though she had lost her personal anchors to the world. The tears began to well up. She turned back to look for some Kleenex. The apartment came equipped with a CD player and a nice collection of classical music but no Kleenex. She tore off a long piece of toilet paper and wadded it up instead.

Julie was at home, Sarah thought, working hard to put her life back in order after what had happened to her. Claire worked hard to simply get through each day. Sarah had left the two people whom she most loved and who most needed her. They were back in Los Angeles while she was here in Paris, thinking about how to fill her time. This was crazy! She had made a terrible mistake.

She blew her nose. She had thought this trip out very carefully before coming. So, no, it was not a mistake. She had promised herself a new beginning and beginnings were hard. It wasn't so crazy to revisit the city she and David had loved, to recall the excitement of those early years of their marriage and—to let them go.

She looked at her watch—almost noon. She needed to get out. The streets beckoned. Paris lay outside her door.

# 14

Sarah walked to the Champs du Mar and watched children playing games and adults of all ages sitting or lying on the ground, some enjoying picnics and others napping in the sun. She walked up and down the streets of the neighborhoods near her apartment and found cheese stores and bakeries—shop windows filled with all manner of delicacies. When her legs grew tired she stopped at an outdoor café for coffee and a roll. She thought how nice it would be to cook a proper meal with all the ingredients she had seen that day. She had purchased a small baguette and some eggs and cheese but she would hardly attempt a special dinner for herself. Then she had an idea. She would invite Michel Vannerie to dinner tomorrow night! Perhaps he would be busy, tomorrow *was* Saturday after all, but then maybe Sunday. All right, she thought, the first thing was to get his number and call. Sarah oriented herself, looking up then down the street, deciding how to get back to 17 Avenue Souffren.

Once inside, she went to the dining room table where a pile of papers had accumulated. She thumbed through the pile; at the bottom was the file Michel had left for her. She pulled out a piece of paper that was clipped to the front cover and picked up the telephone next to the lavender velvet sofa.

"Michel? This is Sarah Coleman. I'm doing well, thank you. Umm, I know this is short notice but I wondered if you would like to come over for dinner tomorrow evening? I like to cook, and I would love to have someone to cook for! You would? How about seven-thirty? Yes? Wonderful. A bientôt."

The following morning, Sarah started out early. She carried a large canvas tote bag to do her errands. She wore khaki pants and flats with a blue-and-white striped cotton T-shirt and a navy sweater tied around her shoulders. She had on no makeup with the exception of some lip gloss; large dark sunglasses covered her eyes. She glanced at herself in a shop window and thought, for a brief moment, that she looked like she belonged in Paris.

She stopped in front of a butcher shop. The meats and poultry were laid out on white paper behind the glass. Everything looked exceptionally fresh. She went inside and, after some discussion with the balding but distinguished looking butcher in his white jacket and apron, decided to purchase a small boneless leg of lamb. He would tie it into a roast for her and keep it so she could pick it up on her way back since, he warned, lugging it around could get heavy! And what did she plan to serve it with? He suggested small fingerling potatoes and fresh asparagus. He even told her how to cook it—she would need a nice white head of garlic and fresh rosemary. Sarah thought about her house in Woodland Hills and how they had planted an herb garden a couple of years in a row.

Sarah looked at the name 'Claude' embroidered on his breast pocket. He *looked* like a Claude with the fringe of hair over his ears, large wire-rim aviator glasses and an ample stomach that pulled at the buttons of his jacket. "Vous êtes Américaine, n'est-ce pas?" he asked.

"Oui," said Sarah. "Parlez-vous Anglais, Monsieur Claude?"

"Bien entendu—of course!" said Claude, "but not well," he added. "You give me some time to practice?"

"Yes, if you will agree to help me with my French," Sarah said with a smile.

"Your husband, he speaks French?" Claude asked as he picked out a nice pink leg of lamb. Sarah did not answer immediately. He must have seen the slim gold band still on her finger.

"I'm here by myself," said Sarah. "My husband died over a year ago. I plan to stay in Paris for a month and I'm cooking dinner tonight for a young Parisian who has been kind to me." The words tumbled out as fast as she could speak them.

"Of this I am glad to hear," said Claude, his back to Sarah. He carefully boned the leg with a sharp, curved knife. "Many Americans say Paris is not a friendly city."

"I've never understood that," said Sarah.

"This is because you try to speak our language I think."

Claude turned around after several moments of waiting and showed Sarah his work with justifiable pride: a perfectly boned leg, criss-crossed with white string. "And because—I don't know how to say it in English—you have the appearance of a nice person."

"Merci, Claude."

"Don't forget to come back for your roast!" he called after her. She waved her hand as she walked out of the store. There was a produce market two blocks further up the street. Outside, tucked in wooden crates, onions and artichokes, strawberries and lemons lay next to each other, nestled in tissue like small treasures. Late spring green and pale white asparagus spears were tied in bunches and stood upright on the right hand side of the display. She walked through the door and found the produce aisle stocked with fresh herbs of all kinds and resolved to buy a few small pots to grow on the balcony that faced the Avenue Souffren.

Sarah walked to the corner and turned left, not sure if this was the direction of the bakery she had seen the day before. Just then she spotted the yellow-and-white striped awning with the words 'Pâtisserie d'Annie' written across the top. Inside the shop the smells of butter, yeast, chocolate and vanilla combined into a heavenly aroma.

"Une baguette, s'il vous plaît," Sarah told the girl behind the counter who picked one out, wrapped it in white paper and handed it to Sarah.

"One euro," the girl said, exaggerating the 'one'. Sarah wondered if she simply *looked* like an American.

"I would also like to buy a dessert for this evening," Sarah said. "What would you recommend? For two people. The tarts look nice."

"Les tartes abricots—they are very good," the girl said, brightening somewhat. "They have a marzipan layer. We are known for our tartes, Madame."

Engage people. Inquire. Try to draw them out, absorb whatever they have to offer. This would be her approach to living in Paris, Sarah decided, though it could work anywhere.

Once home, Sarah hunted through the CD collection to find music to cook by. She chose an album of Vivaldi guitar concertos, and a classic recording of Maria Callas arias. She had a similar recording at home. The melodies created a perfect atmosphere as she seasoned the lamb, preheated the oven and rinsed the small potatoes. She trimmed the asparagus stalks and placed them in a jar of water on the red Formica counter, then she poured herself a glass of wine.

I should call Julie, she reminded herself, but decided to wait until later. She once again thought of David and their trip to Paris ten years ago. She peeled and sliced the garlic inserting the small pieces into tiny slits she'd made in the roast. She rubbed the remaining garlic and rosemary over the outside of the lamb. As the wine relaxed her and the music soared the tears began to fall again. Oh, God, I *must* be able to do this! Otherwise I might as well go back to L.A. She inhaled the fresh aromas of the feast she was assembling. She knew it would only improve with cooking, that the smells would combine and make the apartment seem like home.

A fresh breeze blew in through the small open window in the kitchen. She was preparing this meal because she needed to create *something* that day that would be appreciated and savored and consumed. She would concentrate on these simple tasks and not think about tomorrow or the rest of the month or whether any of what she had chosen to do this summer made sense.

Sarah hastily showered and applied some makeup and found a somewhat wrinkled pair of black pants to wear. The apartment *did* smell heavenly. She found some cloth napkins and a tablecloth and set the table. She had forgotten to buy flowers. Oh well, she just hoped it would be a nice dinner.

The doorbell rang at twenty to eight. Sarah was grateful for the extra ten minutes and with a deep breath, opened the door.

Michel stood in the hallway holding a bottle of red wine and wearing a broad smile and a slouchy leather jacket. For a minute Sarah didn't know whether to lean over and kiss him on each cheek or shake his hand. The issue was settled when Michel reached out his free hand to her in greeting. "Bonsoir, Madame," he said.

"Please call me Sarah! Come in. What a lovely bottle of wine. It will go perfectly with our meal." She turned and he followed her into the apartment.

"Something smells wonderful," said Michel. "You say the cooking pleases you? My mother as well enjoys it, she is a marvelous cook." Sarah smiled briefly, acknowledging that this handsome young man could easily be her son.

"I have a small bottle of Champagne for les aperitifs," she said, feeling unsure of herself. Was she making too big a deal of this evening?

"Would you open it?" Sarah asked. "I wanted to celebrate making my first real dinner in the apartment. And, oh, we are having lamb for the main course. So you can see how your Bordeaux is perfect."

Sarah handed him the split of Champagne. The tiny kitchen was fully equipped and included wine glasses and champagne flutes. She took out two of each and, after expertly popping the cork, Michel filled their glasses and proposed a toast.

"Bienvenue à Paris," he said.

His welcome reminded her of the taxi driver who had driven her in to the city from Charles de Gaulle.

"Merci, Michel," she said.

They sipped Champagne and nibbled on some pate and olives. "I hope I'll have a chance to meet your parents."

"It is possible," said Michel. "In fact they have made friends with many of the Americans who stay in the apartment over the years. Both of my parents were professeurs, like me," he went on. "When they retire, they put advertisement in the magazines of some of the universities in the States. We have mostly academics who rent here, sometimes to attend a conference, or to lecture at the Sorbonne. We introduce them to friends of my parents. It becomes a nice exchange. One time, my parents went to stay with a friend who lives in Palo Alto. He teaches at Stanford and his wife is an artist. They also visit San Francisco. I would love to see it myself. These friends from California, they also rented the house of my Aunt Pauline, you remember? En Provence? They stayed a month last October."

Sarah tossed the salad while Michel poured the wine and helped Sarah carve the lamb. Sarah observed his manners and decided he was raised well. Apart from his looks he seemed older than thirty.

"And you, Michel?"

"Me?"

"Yes. What is a handsome young man like you doing alone on a Saturday night? Even though I'm endlessly grateful you are. This is such a treat for me. Shopping and cooking in my own place in Paris reminds me of all the things I like to do best."

"Je m'excuse," Michel said as he stood up and walked over to the windows.

"I'm sorry," she said. "That was terribly rude of me."

"It is all right," he said slowly.

He sat back down and emptied his wine glass. The Vivaldi guitar concertos played softly. This was a sensitive person, concluded Sarah, someone who has been hurt or disappointed in love.

Michel lifted his face. "I had a girlfriend—Yvonne was her name. We live together for one year. She moves out about one month now. She is a graduate student—not one of mine. We met through friends. She studies Anthropology. I thought we would marry this summer. I would like to have a family. But Yvonne does not want children. She want to travel, to study, to write. Like Margaret Mead, I think!"

"I see."

"So, I have the free night. I am happy you invite me to a real dinner. The roast lamb was excellent. Better than my mother's. But you may not say this when you meet her!"

"Not a word—even though I'm sure that's not true." They sat quietly for a minute as the guitar melodies filled the air. Sarah rose to clear the table. Michel followed her with dishes in both hands.

"Merci," said Sarah, "but no dishwashing! I will make us some coffee. And we have a dessert."

Michel ate a large slice of apricot tart while Sarah sipped espresso. She looked at his face, the strong bones and the sharp line of his jaw. He was quite beautiful, and again she thought of Julie, of her injuries and her diminished aspirations. She wondered if they would like one another if they ever did meet.

"You know, many of my parents' friends are also my friends," said Michel. "La Sorbonne, it is a small town really, inside a large city. I am invited to a dinner party next Friday night. I was not planning to go, but if you like to accompany me, I should accept. I think it will be nice for you to meet some people—well—of your age—in Paris."

Sarah laughed. "It would," she said.

Even though she was tired, Sarah wanted to call Julie and find out how the little troupe was doing in Claire's apartment. It was two-thirty in Los Angeles. Claire should be home from her Saturday hair appointment. Sarah sat down with her coffee and waited for the call to go through.

Asya answered. Julie was out.

"How are you all doing? How is Mother?"

"Ah, we are fine," said Asya. "Julie I no think she likes my cooking. She goes to the store and gets different food. I don't know. Claire, she likes. She no understand Julie. We just get back from Lucille. Your mother, she is beauty now. You want talk to her?"

Sarah shut her eyes for a moment.

"Sure, Asya, that would be good," she said. Sarah could hear Asya tell Claire "It's your daughter!"

"Hi," Claire answered the phone, breathing into it, the acknowledgment of Sarah's presence on the other end audible in her voice.

"Hi, Mom, how are you?"

"Yes," Claire answered, drawing out the yes.

"It's nice to have Julie with you for a little while, isn't it? You three girls! I can just picture it."

Claire laughed and then launched into a series of sentences that Sarah couldn't comprehend, becoming more agitated as she went on. Sarah wished she was able to fathom even the tiniest piece of what Claire was trying to communicate, but she could not. Often Sarah would pretend to understand Claire, injecting a "hmm" or an "Uh-huh". The method occasionally backfired.

"Really?" Sarah said, when Claire paused.

It was an obviously inappropriate response because Claire said, "No!"

"Do, do," Claire implored, not speaking into the receiver. Asya took the phone from her.

"I don't know what this is," said Asya. "She was fine a minute ago. She's calm, we have good day. She looks beauty. Now, I don't know. She's upset!" Asya now seemed agitated as well.

"I'm sorry," said Sarah. "I'll call back tomorrow. Maybe you can find out what the problem is."

"I think it is something with Julie and her room. This is not so neat. It make Claire nervous."

"I'll talk to Julie about it," said Sarah.

"Good," said Asya. "Thank you."

# 15

Sunday morning Sarah woke early. She drew back the curtains in the bedroom and looked up and down the empty sidewalk. Wrapping a chenille robe around her waist she walked into the kitchen to make coffee only to find the remains of the dinner dishes piled in the sink. Sarah had refused Michel's repeated offers to help her clean up and had nudged him out of the kitchen and the apartment after they had finished dessert. Her cheek muscles had ached from the effort she'd made to smile and appear lighthearted throughout the evening.

Sarah had not eaten very much of the meal she had cooked the night before and the wine had left her with a bit of a headache. Coffee and toast, she thought, spying the last of the baguette, and maybe an egg. Sarah stood on tiptoes in order to see as much as she could out of the small window that overlooked the city. Sacre Coeur gleamed white in the morning sun. Its beauty made her sad.

The coffee was ready and Sarah inhaled its aroma. The day ahead of her unfolded like a new map. She would eat breakfast, then take the Métro to Sacre Coeur. She had never been to Montmartre. She would call Julie when she got back and check in on Claire. She had to remind herself that, since the stroke, her mother's bad moods blew over as quickly as they descended.

The walls of the stairwell leading from the Métro stop at Montmartre to the street above were every inch covered with paintings. They were not very good paintings—one stop short of graffiti—but done with such verve and color and spirit that Sarah, breathless, having to pause on the landings because of the steep and endless stairs, smiled at the sight of them.

By the time she reached the open air she had become accustomed to the darkness of the stairwell and the light momentarily blinded her. She put on dark glasses and ventured out. She was not alone in her desire to visit Sacre Coeur and found it easily by following the small clusters of tourists and families and watching for the signs pointing the way to the church. As she approached it she saw she would have to climb yet another long flight of steps. Stopping for a moment she prepared for this last ascent. Bells tolled sounding inevitable and timeless. Sarah pulled a silk scarf out of her purse and tied it beneath her chin. As she climbed the stairs she heard strains of organ music, Gregorian melodies and the sweet sound of feminine voices.

Once inside the church, she took a moment to adjust to the dim light then found a seat at the back, close to the entrance. The interior was simple, almost austere, and relatively unadorned for its size and renown. Two rows of nuns in pale gray habits stood at the front of the Nave. They were singing. The church was half empty. There was a scattering of women and couples who looked as though they might be visitors, interlopers like Sarah. The ancient music—alternating between major and minor keys—enlivened the otherwise solemn quiet and added to the sense of holiness and mystery.

Sarah, a bit awkward, not Catholic but Jewish, knelt on the leather pad and prayed for her tiny family, for guidance, and a kind of grace.

By six in the evening Sarah was back at 17 Avenue Suffren. It had been a good day but a long one. She opened the refrigerator and looked inside. She had eaten a late lunch at a café in Montmartre and wasn't hungry. She pulled out a bottle of white wine and poured herself a glass. She opened the French doors to the balcony, and, braced and sobered by the chill of the evening, decided she would stay in for the rest of the night and go to bed early.

Sarah tried Los Angeles again. This time Julie answered the phone.

"Hi, Julie," said Sarah.

"Hi, Mom."

"How is it going there? I called yesterday but you were out. Grandma was in a state about something. Asya said it might have to do with your room."

"Grandma has her routines," said Julie. "She can't stand to have one thing out of place. She didn't used to be like this. My room isn't bad, especially since every drawer is stuffed full of her things—the closet too."

"Maybe you and Asya can do some spring cleaning. Mother has clothes and shoes that she never wears. It would be good to go through all of that. I'd been meaning to do it myself."

"Yeah, maybe. If Grandma lets us. Sounds like a *lot* of fun. I guess I could take some of the stuff over to the Center or the Women's Shelter."

"That sounds like a great idea. How are things at the Center working out?" Sarah asked.

"All right, I guess, especially since I don't have to drive over the hill every day. The people in the Santa Monica Center are OK. I've been working part-time answering their phones."

"Really good, Julie," said Sarah. Then she added, "By the way, Asya thinks you don't like her cooking."

"I don't," said Julie.

"Try and understand -"

Julie interrupted, "Now you're giving me advice? All the way from Paris?"

"Julie..."

There was a momentary silence, then Sarah spoke again. "Have you thought some more about coming to stay with me? The apartment is quite nice—and, I miss you. We could have fun here, I think."

"Not sure how much 'fun' I'd be but I guess I'll check into flights. Are you still planning to go to the south of France?"

"I'm not sure. A relative of the people who own this apartment has a farmhouse in Provence. It does sound intriguing."

"What if I meet you there instead?" suggested Julie, sounding grown up. "I want to spend a few more weeks in L.A. I still go over to see Tammy once a week. We're talking about my feelings about what happened and what I'm going to do about work and I don't know—everything."

"All right, but if you want to come sooner, just let me know. You have my number, right? And e-mail. I check it often."

"OK, Mom."

"I love you, sweetheart," Sarah said.

"Love you too, bye."

Sarah felt very tired, yet relieved that she wouldn't have to deal with Julie's moods quite yet. The thought made her feel guilty. She chose not to dwell on it. She got ready for bed, crawled under the covers and was soon asleep.

That night Sarah had a dream. She was at a party with a number of sophisticated Parisians. There was drinking and laughter and loud music. A door opened and Julie walked in. The laughter dwindled and the music stopped. Everyone turned to look. Julie wore torn clothes. Her hair was disheveled, her face bruised and the red lipstick on her mouth was smeared. Sarah felt embarrassed. The heat of her embarrassment colored her face but she tried to appear pleased at the sight of her daughter. She introduced Julie to the guests in French. Julie said nothing. The guests asked Julie questions but she did not understand them. The questions were delivered in staccato fashion, like gunfire. Julie looked stunned, vulnerable. Sarah understood, all at once, that Julie was in imminent danger. She tried to move Julie away from the group, so they could speak privately, but the others gathered closer to Julie and began, affectionately at first, to touch her bruises, her lips. They ran their hands through her tangled hair and pulled at her torn blouse and skirt. Sarah, terrified, realized that she was responsible for Julie's predicament. She screamed for Julie to follow her and grabbed Julie's arm to lead her away. But Julie was cemented to the spot, no longer a 24 year old but younger, a child in fact. The crowd was poised to devour her when Sarah awoke. It was barely six in the morning but she was unable to fall back asleep. She decided to get up and begin the day, letting her dream dissolve into daylight.

Sarah pulled open the drapes that covered the French windows in the living room and looked out to overcast skies.

The granite building across the street was older and more elegant than the one in which Sarah was staying. Its windows were decorated with graceful and freshly painted black wrought iron and many had planters spilling over with red geraniums. The drapes were open in one of the apartments and she could see a honey-colored grand piano inside. No one was playing it. Sarah observed the sky above the rooftops. It was clogged with fat, threatening clouds and through the open window the air smelled like rain.

J.S. Tyndall

That day and for the rest of the week, Sarah explored Paris. One morning was spent at the Musée Picasso with its small but spectacular collection of paintings and the haunting, ethereal pieces made especially for the museum by Giacommetti—light fixtures, impractical benches and tables. After the museum, she walked through the Marais toward the lushly green and symmetrical Place des Voges, stopping at Joe Goldenberg's, the oldest delicatessen in Paris, famous for its corned beef sandwiches. Sarah sat at one of their outdoor tables, the sun warm on her face, and ate one on a thin crusty roll. Another day she strolled through the arrondissements close to her apartment all the way to La Coupole where she sipped a café crème and watched beautiful people smoke endless cigarettes and pick at their food. They never seemed to run out of amusing things to talk about. Before leaving, Sarah bought a small milk pitcher with 'La Coupole' painted on it to add to her collection packed carefully away at Northridge Moving and Storage.

# 16

By Friday, Sarah was anxious about the party. How long had it been since she'd gone to one not associated with work? This will be *nice*, she tried to reassure herself, as she ran a bath and sprinkled lavender bath salts—bought at one of the local outdoor markets—under the rush of hot water. She soaked a washcloth in the water and held it to her face and neck. What if everyone was younger than she was? When David was alive Sarah was unconcerned with age. Now she was conscious of time passing in a way she had never been before.

Michel said many of the people who would be at the party were friends of his parents so they would have to be at least her age. She thought about what she would wear. Something simple, but what? It had been chilly the last few nights. She would wear a blouse and a long skirt with high-heeled sandals. She would carry a sweater for later. She added some silver bracelets and hoop earrings and pronounced herself dressed. Michel had called that afternoon and told her he would pick her up at seven. She was planning to take a cab, she said, but Michel was adamant.

On the way to the party, Michel asked Sarah about her week and she reported her discoveries to him. Michel slowed down on a leafy street in a quiet residential area. He squeezed his tiny car into a parking space. When they rang the bell a muscular man with thick dark hair opened the door.

"Bonsoir! You must be l'Américaine—Madame Coleman," the man said as he reached for her elbow to guide her inside.

"Please. Call me Sarah," she said in French.

"Ah, bon, Sarah. And I am Jean-Pierre."

Michel and Jean-Pierre gave each other a quick hug. Michel asked how Sylvie was. In the car Michel had explained that Jean-Pierre, their host, was a friend and colleague at the Sorbonne and Sylvie was his wife, an accomplished artist.

The rooms were well lit. A fine crystal vase filled with fresh flowers stood on a rustic, antique chest in the entry hall. The home was decorated in a relaxed manner with a combination of old and modern pieces of furniture, Persian rugs, and wonderfully bold, colorful, paintings on every available wall.

"Excuse, Sarah," said Jean-Pierre. "You would like a drink?"

"I will get it for her," Michel said. With a nod of approval, Jean-Pierre moved off to his other guests.

"He seems very nice," said Sarah.

"Yes. And you will like Sylvie as well. These are her paintings—here," Michel pointed, "and here."

"Amazing," Sarah said.

"Like Sylvie." Michel gestured toward the far wall. Leaning against the doorframe that opened into the kitchen was a tall, large-boned woman in her 50's, throwing her head back in laughter. Her unruly salt and pepper hair swung behind her revealing chandelier-style earrings and a long, still elegant neck. Sylvie was talking with another man who appeared to be older than Sylvie but closer to her age than the artist's husband. Sylvie had married someone younger than she and it struck Sarah as wonderful and unconventional.

"You would like a glass of Champagne?" asked Michel.

"Yes, thank you," answered Sarah, without taking her eyes off Sylvie and the man she was talking to. The man wore glasses and had a pleasant face, a congenial face. Michel noticed this apparent interest and without another word led her toward the impromptu bar where Sylvie and the man stood. It was a simple wooden sideboard laid out with bottles of wine, non-vintage Champagne and sparkling water, near the entrance to the kitchen. Michel kissed Sylvie on both cheeks and shook the man's hand warmly.

"Sylvie, Benjamin, this is Sarah, l'Américaine."

"Hello, Sarah," said Sylvie reaching a long arm from under a shawl she'd tied around her shoulders. Michel filled a glass with Champagne and handed it to Sarah.

"I will be back in a moment," he said and disappeared into the crowd.

The man standing next to Sylvie said, "Hello."

"Bonsoir," said Sarah. Then, before she could think of anything else to say, especially in French, the man awkwardly excused himself and stepped away to the bar. Sarah watched him fill two glasses with white wine and cross the room to a young, attractive woman who appeared to be waiting for him. Sylvie interrupted Sarah's absorption.

"You are enjoying your stay in Paris?" Sylvie asked with a twinkle in her eye.

Sarah felt startled and then embarrassed. She tried to recover by speaking quickly. "Yes, so far. I've walked and walked. The other day I visited the Musée Picasso. It was incredible." Sarah looked at the walls of the house. "Michel told me you did all these paintings and they're *also* wonderful!"

"To be mentioned in the same sentence with Picasso!" Sylvie said, laughing. "Please, feel free to look at them more closely. I see someone to whom I must speak. You will be all right? Michel will be right back, I am certain."

Sarah nodded, then craned her neck to look for Michel. She was not able to locate him. She did, however, see Benjamin, the man she had just met, speaking intently with the young woman. Perhaps she was one of his students, but then this was Paris and anything was possible. A couple came up to the bar and greeted Sarah in French, she responded and they began to speak in a dizzying avalanche of words and phrases she could barely make out. She could feel the Champagne as she emptied her glass. She smiled at the couple apologetically and ducked away.

Wondering when her hosts were to serve dinner, she turned her head toward the kitchen from which emanated the smell of sautéed mushrooms and onions with just the right amount of garlic and tarragon. Sarah breathed in the aromas, shutting her eyes for a moment in anticipation. Suddenly a loud crash and a scream came from that very room, sending Sylvie, Sarah and the couple she had just left running in to the kitchen to see what had occurred.

It seems that Nini, the caterer, had dropped a hot tray of hors d'oeuvres. Nini was a petite girl, not much older than twenty, her dark hair pulled away from her face. She was kneeling on the floor over the spilled appetizers.

"Je suis désolé!" said Nini.

"C'est un accident," said Sylvie reassuringly.

Sarah bent down to help pick up the food but Sylvie shook her head.

"No, please. Here," she said, handing Sarah another tray, "you may help me by passing these to my guests. Nini and I will take care of the kitchen." Sarah's mouth watered as she held the tray of miniature tarts—gruyère, onion, mushroom.

Sarah handed out the last of her platter and returned it to the kitchen. She took two tarts and a napkin from the counter and walked back into the living room where she sat down in a window seat and watched the people at the party. Her eye caught Benjamin's across the room. He was no longer standing with the young woman but was chatting with another older man. Sarah looked away. He was very appealing, she thought. She stood up and pulled on her sweater, preparing to leave.

"Hello again," Benjamin said, appearing in front of her.

"Hello," said Sarah.

"Are you cold, so you need your sweater?"

"I was planning to leave but I must find my bag and call a taxi."

"But why? Please don't go yet. I saw you passing the tray. This was kind of you to help Sylvie. "

"Oh," she said, surprised that he had noticed her.

"You will have a glass of wine with me?"

"Why not," said Sarah. And Benjamin went to the bar to fill his glass and returned with one for Sarah. He nodded at the empty window seat and they sat down together.

"Are you hungry?" he asked.

"Starved!" Sarah said, forgetting how awkward she had felt moments ago.

"One minute," he said. "Don't move!" Benjamin jogged over to the kitchen, dodging other guests and returned with two napkins full of hors d'oeuvres.

"Thank you!" said Sarah.

"So, you stay in Paris for a month? At the Vannerie's apartment?"

"Yes," she said. Then she added, "Where is Michel? I haven't seen him since we arrived."

"He went upstairs. I think he is on the phone with his ex-girl friend. Their break-up has him quite despondent."

"So you know him well," observed Sarah.

"I know his parents and now Michel and I are colleagues and friends at La Sorbonne. I teach law.

"My husband was an estate and tax attorney."

"I thought you are in Paris alone..."

"He died a little more than a year ago."

"I am sorry," he said, looking directly at Sarah. "My wife, Marie, she passed away eight years this summer.

"Oh. I'm sorry too," said Sarah.

"It is a surprise—how it is so final," Benjamin reflected.

"Exactly," she said. They drank their wine and watched the people in the room for a few minutes.

"What kind of law do you teach?" she asked.

"I teach Banking Law—domestic and international," he said. "I have many Americans who study in a joint degree program with Cornell and L'Université de Paris—Sorbonne. The program confers a Matrise en Droit as well as a J.D., the U.S. equivalent."

"I'm surprised by how many people in Paris speak English."

"In Europe, the better schools require at least one and often two additional languages beside one's own native tongue," he explained.

Sarah knew the U.S. was provincial in this regard, or arrogant, depending on one's point of view. "We should do the same," she said.

"You are separated from other countries by large oceans on either side. We have only to drive a few miles. It is understandable."

"How generous," Sarah said. "I thought the French looked down on Americans for this reason, among others."

He laughed. "Maybe only they are envious!"

They continued to talk for a while until Michel joined them. Sarah told Michel she would like to go home but would be happy to take a taxi. Michel said he was ready to leave as well. He went to find Sylvie.

"I must attend a conference in London to give a paper on Thursday. May I call you when I return?"

Sarah's heart pounded. She raced through possible responses. She could think of nothing clever. Yes. Of course she would say yes.

"I would like that very much," she replied with a smile, trying to appear calm.

"All right then," he said. Just then, Michel returned with Sarah's purse.

"Where did you find that?" she asked Michel, standing up.

"Beside my keys," he said. He clasped Benjamin on the shoulder. "Are we going for a bike ride tomorrow?"

"Absolument," said Benjamin who then turned to Sarah and reached out his hand. When she extended hers he held it for an extra moment and she felt a lovely warmth spread throughout her body.

"Good luck with your paper," she said.

"Merci, Sarah. A bientôt."

# 17

On Saturday, Sarah walked along the Seine, crossed it at the Pont d'Alexandre, and continued by foot all the way to the Tuileries. Sunday she went to a concert at L'Eglise Saint-Sulpice for which she had bought a ticket earlier in the week. It was a cello recital given by a young man of Eurasian descent. He played three of the Bach Suites. She loved the Bach Suites and owned a CD of Yo-Yo Ma's famous rendition. She walked up to the young man after the concert and complimented him in French. She hoped he would have a chance to tour in America. He laughed and said he was not good enough yet but perhaps someday—he'd always wanted to visit San Francisco.

Sarah walked all the way back to the apartment—from the Sixth Arrondissment to the Fifteenth. The late daylight faded to dusk. The grand facades of the Hausmann-style buildings etched themselves against the sky, lifting her spirits with their repetitious beauty.

Once she got home she realized she hadn't bought anything to cook for dinner. Most restaurants closed on Sunday evenings in Paris so she made a simple omelet and ate it with the end of a baguette. She read until the clock ticked past twelve, signaling that the weekend was officially over.

By Wednesday, Sarah decided nothing was going to come of it. If Benjamin had wanted to arrange to see her again he could have called before he left for the conference. She felt silly, like a teenager waiting for the phone to ring.

Sarah left home after a bite of lunch and walked to a nearby internet café. She had found one that was clean and well maintained three blocks from the apartment and had used it several times since Michel told her using her laptop would be a problem with no Wi-fi available in the building. She e-mailed both Julie and her friend Sharon. Julie had said she was firming up her plans to come to France. Sarah would have to call Becca for she never checked her mail and Sarah wanted to ask her about Claire.

It was a breezy afternoon. Rain was expected toward the weekend but looked as though it might come sooner than that. The internet café was nearly empty. The girl who was working that day barely looked up from her magazine when Sarah walked in.

"You'll want an American keyboard, yes?" the girl asked.

"Oui, s'il vous plait," answered Sarah.

"Number five. Over there," said the girl pointing toward a vacant station. "One euro for 30 minutes."

"Merci," said Sarah.

Sarah logged on and began to go through her messages. Junk, junk, mostly junk, a bunch of jokes she deleted, unread, a new message from Sharon. But wait—here was something else. She had almost deleted it, not recognizing the sender: *Benjm@ wanadoo.fr.* The subject line read: Le Diner. She clicked on it. It was from Benjamin. She'd forgotten she'd given him her e-mail address along with her phone number, scribbled on a piece of paper he had found in his pocket before they got up from the window seat. When had he written the e-mail? Monday. Monday! *Before* he left for London.

Bonjour Sarah,
I wonder if you would like to have dinner

with me Friday night? I am quite busy
working at the moment so I may not have the
time to call you properly. I hope you will
not take offense. If I do not hear from you
via e-mail then I will call you when I return.
Cordialement,
Benjamin Manet

How sweet, she thought. How romantic and old fashioned. She clicked on 'Reply' and said she would like to have dinner on Friday. She wished him well with his work and signed the note 'A Bientôt'—see you soon.

Sarah sat back in the armless swivel chair and smiled. She scrolled through the remaining messages. Nothing from Julie. She would call her. She read Sharon's message, mostly questions about Paris, then dashed off a note to Julie asking how things were going and promising a phone call later in the day. She looked at her watch. She had been at the terminal just over a half-hour. She'd have to pay for two sessions instead of one. It didn't matter, she felt buoyed. Hopeful. She thought about David and what he would think about her going out with another man. Moreover, what if he knew how much she *wanted* to go?

She handed the euros to the unhappy looking girl who was now talking to a friend on her cell phone. That was it, wasn't it? Most people who were sullen and cross were just unhappy. Sarah felt sorry for the girl—boot black hair with platinum stripes, pinned down with barrettes—nails bitten to reveal pink skin beneath. The girl could have been Julie's age.

The streets of Paris were crowded with office workers getting off in time to pick up a few groceries for dinner: a bottle of wine, a half-priced baguette, chops wrapped in paper. The cafes were full of shoppers taking a late afternoon espresso before going home. Girlfriends met, little dogs at their sides tucked between shopping bags. Lovers walked arm in arm or stood and kissed. No one seemed to notice. Despite the threat of rain, Sarah perceived a buzz in the air, a spring/summer fever she'd caught herself the minute she had slowly, repeatedly read Benjamin's e-mail. She sipped an espresso, seated in a café with mirrors on the walls and caught a glimpse of herself. Her hair was a mess. She still needed a hair cut, preferably before the weekend! But her face—she had to admit her face was aglow.

That evening, Sarah called Julie. She was able to reach her on her cell phone but Julie was working at the reception desk of the Santa Monica Rape Crisis Center and asked if Sarah could call back in ten minutes.

Sarah hung up and put a kettle on to boil for tea. She flipped through the television channels until she found CNN International. There was a breaking news bulletin, but then there was always a breaking news bulletin. This one, however, caught her attention. The London Bureau was reporting an accident at which moment the kettle began to whistle forcing Sarah from the sofa. She brought a mug of hot water with the tea bag steeping in it back to the living room. There had been some kind of explosion in one of the underground tube stations. She waited to see which one. There was footage of blood and wreckage and people running and crying and emergency workers pulling and heaving huge pieces of debris from the tops of victims. It was unknown at this point what had happened. Was it a bomb? It was too soon to tell, the reporter said. It had been rush hour and the trains were jammed to capacity. When the phone rang, Sarah leaned over to get it.

"Hello?" she said.

"I thought you were going to call me back! You know I can't make long distance calls from here. Call me back, OK?" said Julie.

"I'm sorry," Sarah said. "I—I was watching the news and got distracted. Hang up. I'll call right now."

Sarah hung up the phone and looked on the end table for her Filofax, which also had all her numbers in it. For a minute or two she couldn't find it and worried that she had left it somewhere. It was in the kitchen. She'd brought it in with her when she was making the tea. Calm down, she thought. He wouldn't have been in the subway for God's sake, would he? An attorney? But he wasn't a practicing lawyer, he was a teacher. She had to call Julie back, although for a minute she couldn't remember just why.

"Finally," Julie said. "Things are crazy around here. Grandma has a cold and I haven't been able to find a decent air fare to Marseilles and—"

"Hold on, Julie. Everything can't be falling apart," said Sarah, knowing it could.

"You only want to hear good news, right?"

"That's not fair, sweetheart."

"You have to admit you've done everything you could to get as far away from me as possible."

"What? What are you talking about?" Sarah asked.

"I don't know. I'm just having a bad day," Julie said.

"Why don't you go to a travel agency and let them help you. I'm sure there's one close to Grandma's apartment. I'm really looking forward to your visit. I made arrangements to rent the farmhouse in Provence. It will be a chance for us to spend some relaxing time together—and us to become better friends."

"I have friends," Julie said. "What I need is a mother."

Never. I can never say the right thing. "It's OK, Julie. You're stronger than you think. You'll see."

"That's what Tammy's been telling me."

"Tammy's right, honey. Should I call you later?"

"No. But—I'm gonna need some money."

"I can have money wired to your checking account." Then Sarah added, "This will be good for us, Julie," hoping she was even half right.

# 18

Sarah had been in bed reading when the phone startled her with its still unfamiliar double-beep.

"Hello?" she said.

"Bonsoir, Sarah. It is Benjamin Manet. I hope I did not wake you. I should not have telephoned this late."

Benjamin Manet. The sound of his voice electrified her.

"No! I mean—it's all right," she hurried to say. "I was reading. How are you? *Where* are you? Are you back in Paris?"

"Alors. That is why I am calling. I must stay here in London through the morning. I thought I could pass up a panel discussion tomorrow but they need me to fill in for a colleague who had to leave—a family emergency."

"I know all about those," Sarah said. Suddenly she remembered the subway accident. "I—I was worried about you," she said. "The accident in the subway? I wasn't expecting to hear from you but—still—well, I'm glad you're all right."

"Actually, the accident was quite near our hotel. They say it may have been a terrorist action but they are not sure yet. It's so strange—the way things are now. I could have been on that train."

"I didn't know if you rode the Tube," said Sarah.

"Mais oui! London taxis are horribly expensive."

"Thank you for calling, she said. "We can have dinner another time."

"Mais non," he said, "we don't have to cancel. I should be back by six. What if I picked you up at 8:45? It would give me time to shower and change. I know of a wonderful bistro not far from you. L'Etoile. I can make a 9:00 reservation."

Sarah smiled. "Why don't you let me do it? It's a local call."

"Merci," he said. "But perhaps use my name. The owner is a friend."

Benjamin picked Sarah up in one of the tiny cars that were ubiquitous on the streets of Paris. He had called to let her know he would wait in front for her since securing a parking place at that time of night was difficult if not impossible. Benjamin jumped out and ran to the passenger side to open the door for her.

"What a darling car," said Sarah.

"It's new. It gets fantastic gas mileage, which is why everyone has them; that and the fact that parking spaces in Paris are at a premium. The smaller the better—not like your American—what do you call them?—SVU's?"

"SUV's!" Sarah laughed. "And I had one so don't say bad things about them. I loved mine but now I have a small car too."

"Good for you—oh—here we are," Benjamin said, stopping in front of the restaurant with its black awning. "Why don't you let them know we are here? I'll park the car and meet you inside."

"All right," Sarah said.

The maitre'd seated Sarah at a nice corner table and a waiter brought menus and a wine list. Sarah watched the door. When Benjamin came in he searched the room. Upon seeing her he smiled broadly and made his way to their table. He was dressed in a navy sport coat and khaki pants and looked especially professorial. He was not wearing a tie but his button down, blue-

and-white checked shirt was flattering and as he sat down she could see his blue eyes twinkle behind his glasses.

"We shall have wine?" he asked.

"Of course!" said Sarah, handing him the wine list.

He looked it over, then closed it and signaled for the waiter. "You like a nice, white wine? They have excellent fish and seafood—here."

"Perfect," said Sarah.

"Ce Montrachet, ci," Benjamin said, pointing to a wine on the list.

"Bon, merci Monsieur Manet," said the waiter and went off to get their wine.

"I guess you come here quite a bit," said Sarah, wondering how many women he had brought to this place.

"Marie and I used to come here often. Now I come mainly with visitors."

"Visiting professors?" asked Sarah.

"Yes," he said.

"I know all about visitors. I work at a university, in a law school—Kelton Hall in Los Angeles."

"I have heard of it," he said.

"It's a very good law school, and getting better all the time."

"What do you do there? You are not an attorney, or at least you only mentioned your husband."

"No, I'm not. I help the school raise money."

"That is interesting," said Benjamin, nodding to the waiter who had returned with the bottle. "We could use this in France. The universities are badly in need of funds and the government cannot afford to support us the way they have in the past. It really is a crisis."

"It used to be only the private schools in the U.S. that would raise money for scholarships or endowments or for new buildings," said Sarah, "but now the public schools have to do it as well—for the same reasons you mention."

"Try your wine," he said, raising his glass. "Sante," he said.

"Sante. Mmm, it's delicious," said Sarah.

"So, you have been doing this a long time? Raising money for the law school?"

"Twelve years," said Sarah. "But I'm on leave right now—a kind of sabbatical you might say."

"I'm glad you chose Paris," Benjamin said, looking at her from behind his glasses.

"Me too," said Sarah, feeling a blush rise on her neck and face.

"You look lovely, Sarah." he said.

"Merci." She looked down at the menu.

"The chef," said Benjamin, "he revises the menu daily. Tonight, I notice they are serving a John Dory with asparagus and a beurre blanc sauce. How does that sound?"

"It sounds wonderful," said Sarah.

Once Benjamin gave the waiter their order they sipped their wine and watched the other diners.

"This place is near the Bois de Boulogne," said Benjamin. "You have been there?"

"Not on this trip. Before though, when David and I were here last. We went to a small museum near the park. I can't remember the name but I remember the lower level was filled with paintings by Monet."

"Le Marmotton!" he said. "It is a treasure of which there are so many in Paris. Still, I am surprised you find this one."

"Your name," said Sarah, "Manet..."

"I am no relation to the painter Edouard Manet—at least not that I know of. It is not an unusual name in France. He was a great painter as well. You have been to the Musée D'Orsay?"

"Only once—on that last trip. I need to make sure I go there before I leave Paris."

"We could go there together if you like. How much longer are you here?"

"Two weeks," said Sarah. "And, yes, that would be very nice—I mean I would love to go with you." Sarah blushed again, adding a deep rose undertone to her complexion. The teal-colored shawl she had pulled over her bare shoulders enhanced the color of her eyes and the soft lighting flattered her skin.

Without speaking, Benjamin extended his hand and Sarah took it and held it. The touch of his skin thrilled her and awakened a physical desire she had not felt in a long time.

They eagerly devoured their first course—a salad of baby lettuces, smoky peppers and crumbled Roquefort cheese—along with the delicious, crusty rolls that were served with chilled sweet butter.

"You told me your son teaches at Berkeley, isn't that right?" Sarah asked once the salad plates were cleared.

"Yes," said Benjamin. "His name is Phillipe. We are very close. His wife is pregnant with their first child—my first grandchild. Marie—" he paused and looked at Sarah.

Sarah shook her head. "She was your wife and Phillipe's mother. Of course you would think of her."

"I do not always look back," he said, "but when I think of how happy she would have been to have had a grandchild. This is something different. You understand?"

"Of course," said Sarah. Benjamin talked about his son and his family and his affection for California until the waiter brought their main course.

"The food here is exquisite—delicious!" Sarah exclaimed. "You say you know the owner? Is he also the chef?"

"Yes to both of your questions," Benjamin said.

"I would like to try and prepare this dish," said Sarah, studying her plate. It would all depend on the fish, naturally."

"You like to cook?" He asked.

"I do. It relaxes me. It has always been my—I don't know—my creative outlet I guess. I used to love to experiment with new recipes when David and Julie lived at home." There it was again—the past, restored to perfection, untouchable.

"How lucky for them. I will ask Alain for this recipe. He is not in the restaurant tonight or else he would have already come out to see us. I think he is in New York. His sous chef is quite young but also very talented. Alain trains his sous chefs and they go on to open their own places in the end. It is a difficult business."

"I have thought about taking some cooking classes while I'm in France."

"Merveilleuse," said Benjamin. "I like to cook but do not spend the time it takes to become good at it." He paused for a minute. "You know there is an excellent école de cuisine—a school—in Mausanne-les-Alpilles, the place where Michel's aunt has her home."

Sarah put her fork down and looked at him. "I know—I have looked in to this school. You see, I've been trying to decide about renting Pauline's mas. Michel suggested it when I first arrived in Paris."

"Michel mentioned this to me. I have been there often."

"Is it lovely?" asked Sarah.

"It is. It's very old and the property is beautiful. Pauline has a cherry orchard."

"I don't know. I must get back to them. It's only two weeks away. I'm thinking of renting it for a month and having Julie, my daughter, come to stay with me for part of the time."

"I think you should do it!" he said.

"You do?" Sarah asked.

"Absolument. Without a doubt."

They shared a light sorbet for dessert, and sipped espresso. It had begun to rain outside, and they watched diners departing the restaurant scurry to get in their cars.

"Sarah, how would you like to go to the Musée D'Orsay with me one day next week?"

"I'd like it very much," Sarah said.

"What about Wednesday?" he asked, after checking a calendar he carried in the pocket of his sport coat.

"If I were home I would have a calendar to consult but as it is..."

"I take it that is a 'yes'?"

"Yes," said Sarah.

"Good. I will telephone tomorrow."

Sarah thought about the next day, Sunday. She had no plans that day either.

As if reading her mind, Benjamin said, "You know, the Musée is open on Sundays but it is always very crowded this day with everyone off work."

"Wednesday is better for me," said Sarah, thinking it might be all right to have some space between them, not sure what to make of her jumble of feelings yet.

"All right then, Wednesday," he said.

J.S. Tyndall

From under the canopy, outside the restaurant, Sarah and Benjamin looked out at the street—the slick pavements and the pouring rain. Neither one of them had an umbrella. They looked at each other and Benjamin pulled Sarah to him.

"I will get the car," he said, as though he were whispering something more intimate. Sarah turned to look into his eyes and reached her arms around his neck. He was trembling as he bent to kiss her. The kiss was full of promise. It left Benjamin's glasses tilted on his nose. Sarah smiled at the thought of their first kiss on a rainy Paris sidewalk. It was the kind of thing that only happened in movies.

# 19

Benjamin called Sarah late on Sunday to confirm their date for Wednesday. He told her how busy he would be early in the week but that he was looking forward to the Musée D'Orsay and to seeing her again. Sarah spent most of the day doing laundry and puttering around the apartment. It had showered on and off all morning, but it had partially cleared by the early afternoon. She decided to hurry out to the internet café to check her mail. Julie sent an e-mail that proposed her travel arrangements. If Sarah still planned to be in Provence, Julie could arrive one week after Sarah got there. Would Sarah be able to pick her up at the airport in Marseilles? She would be flying on Air France and gave Sarah some tentative dates and times. Sarah jotted down the particulars on a piece of scratch paper. Julie went on to say that Claire had not been feeling well and that she worried about leaving her. She is her mother's daughter, thought Sarah with a little smile. She would try and reach Julie by phone that evening. She would tell her that Claire was not Julie's problem! She needed to speak with Asya and Becca as well. She had thought about catching an American movie on the Champs Elysee, but decided instead to go back to the apartment. She was existing in a kind of reverie as she thought about the previous evening with Benjamin. Leaving the internet café she passed couples walking together and imagined what it would be like if she and Benjamin made love.

Sarah tried Becca first because Chicago was two hours closer in time to Paris and because Becca was always up early.

"Hi, Becca, it's Sarah."

"How is your grand adventure going?"

"Fine. Great, in fact. I just received an email from Julie though. She said Claire is still not better. She probably needs to see Dr. Blooming. Have you spoken with Asya?"

"I just got off the phone with her. Mother's having difficulty breathing—complications from the upper respiratory infection she had last week. I already phoned Blooming's office. He's on call this weekend so he should be getting back to me soon."

"Good. Hopefully it's nothing serious."

"Hopefully it's nothing that requires a hospital," Becca said, sounding weary.

"No kidding. Every time she goes in, she comes out weaker and less resilient. Remember last December when she ended up with bronchitis?"

"Yes," said Becca. "I can't remember if that's when the doctors decided to put her on inhalation therapy."

"It was. Twice a day. Thank God Asya knows all about things like that."

"It's her job," said Becca.

"We're not paying her a nurse's salary. In fact I think we should give her a raise."

"She has a terrific set-up. An apartment across from the ocean, all of her expenses paid."

"I don't think you realize how lucky we are to have Asya. She has become a friend to Mom. She's her best friend, really. Fanny and Ruth still call but it's not the same as it was. I know."

"Of course you do," said Becca. Her tone was chilly. "You've *been* there and I haven't."

"Becca, you live in Chicago. I'm not blaming you for that— how could I? But I've seen what Asya does. We need to show her how much we appreciate her." Sarah couldn't understand why Becca took Asya's excellent care for granted. "Did I ever tell you what Asya said to me?" asked Sarah.

"What—there have been a lot of things."

"One time when I was concerned about Mother's behavior, when she had been particularly uncooperative about something, I told Asya that I hoped she would stay with us a long time and she looked at me and said, 'Sarah, I'm here until the end.'"

"You did tell me," said Becca.

"Oh," Sarah paused. "And what about you? Are you all right?" asked Sarah.

"I guess—I don't know. Mark is acting strange. He's gone to the annual meeting. It's in Baltimore. He couldn't wait to get on the plane."

"Excited to go to a convention of dentists?"

"Exactly," sighed Becca.

"Maybe you both should come visit me in Provence. I mean there won't be enough room at the house if Julie comes but—"

"You haven't told me about Provence."

"No? I thought I had," replied Sarah. "Julie's going to meet me there for the last three weeks of my stay."

"Well, in answer to your question, *we* won't be coming to Europe. Mark doesn't seem to want to travel these days—"

"But you just said—"

"I mean with me," clarified Becca.

"Oh," said Sarah.

"Yeah," said Becca. "Listen, Dr. Blooming's on the other line."

"Go. We'll talk later."

"OK," Becca said and hung up.

"I'm here until the end," Asya had said. Sarah knew what a precious commitment that was, especially if it were true.

She went into the kitchen and pulled the sheets out of the miniscule washing machine. She could barely fit them in the matching dryer but was glad she could clean them at home. She had found service of any kind in Paris to be phenomenally expensive.

It had begun to rain again, and the wind blew the window in the kitchen shut, the tiny, high window that faced Sacre Coeur. The white cathedral was hidden behind clouds. It was an afternoon to stay indoors. If only, Sarah thought, she wasn't alone. It would be so nice to share this rainy afternoon with someone—like Benjamin for instance. But was she ready for that kind of thing? Was she ready to take the kind of risk she had been avoiding since David? He was, after all, still a stranger, even though they had—that kiss. She had not expected herself to like him—or anyone—as much as she did. Well, she thought, don't get carried away. At the most, it might turn into a summer romance. Or not, she concluded, as summer romances were the stuff of love songs – or novels.

# 20

They had agreed to meet at the museum on Wednesday. The morning air was fresh, cooled from the recent rains. If Sarah had not been running late she might have walked the distance from her apartment.

As she emerged from the Métro stop near the Musée D'Orsay she felt her chest pound. It was *not* because of the many stairs she had just climbed but from her excited heart. Sarah smiled when she spotted Benjamin off to one side of the museum entrance, his head in a book. He didn't notice her until she was right in front of him. Standing to greet her with a kiss on each cheek, he reached for her hand and squeezed it. The gesture was touching, proprietary. You are with me, it told her.

They walked into the building and stood together, hand in hand, taking in the enormous length of the nave with its huge gilt-and-iron clock hanging high on the opposite wall.

"I can almost see the trains chugging into the station," Sarah said.

Benjamin pointed to the main floor. "Think of this space as a huge tunnel through which the trains entered and left the station. It must have been a noisy, smoky place back then."

"When was it turned into a museum?" Sarah asked.

"Quite a long while after it was closed to the trains," he answered. "You see, the tracks here were not of a length to accommodate the more modern engines and their higher speeds. Eventually only trains to and from the suburbs arrived here and then, finally, the Gare was shuttered. At one point it was to have been torn down completely."

"That would've been terrible!"

"You are right," Benjamin said. "In the end, however, the government declared D'Orsay a landmark. It was 1971, I think, after plans had already been designed by Le Corbusier for a modern hotel on the site! Years later, it was decided that the station should be turned into a museum that would house the great works of the 19th Century, forming a kind of artistic bridge between the Louvre and the Centre Georges Pompidou. Thus it is the home, most famously, of the Impressionists and those artists who closely preceded and followed them."

Sarah laughed and said, "Shall we see some of those paintings now?"

"I am boring you?"

"Hardly," she said, slipping her arm through his. He pressed his arm down over Sarah's and she smiled at him.

They took the elevator directly to the fourth floor, home to the Impressionists. They walked through the rooms hand in hand, letting go only to read the curatorial notes of a particular painting or discuss what they saw—the Monets, the Renoirs and finally Manet's, "Olympia" and the elegant portrait of his sister-in-law, Berthe Morisot.

"You're sure Edouard's not a distant relative of yours?" Sarah asked in a teasing voice.

"My family does not think so," Benjamin said, studying the painting of Morisot. "But who knows? I think he and I are moved by a similar beauty," he said, looking at Sarah. "You resemble her, I think!"

Sarah raised her eyebrows. "Merci monsieur, but she looks much more like my daughter, Julie, with her dark hair and eyes."

"I read somewhere that Morisot's eyes were actually green—like yours."

They spent another hour with the Impressionists, moving on to Van Gogh and Cézanne.

"I'm starved," she said, as they left the room with the Cézannes in it.

"Let us go to the café then," Benjamin said.

The small Museum Café overlooked the Seine through huge arched and paned windows. Sarah ordered a salade du chef and a glass of white wine while Benjamin had a roll and coffee.

"I've never taken a boat ride on the Seine," she said, looking out at the river through the windows of the café. "On the the—what are they called?"

"Bateaux Mouches? Yes, you can go down to the river banks at almost any hour and have a boat ride. It is a lovely day. Shall we go after lunch?"

"Could we?" she asked.

"Pourquoi pas?" he answered. Why not? "It is a good way to experience Paris, le vieux Paris, the oldest part of the city."

"Can you spare the time away from your work?" she asked, sipping her wine.

He looked at her an smiled. "This day is for us," he said.

She reached her hand out to him across the table and he took it.


As the boat plied its way slowly through the waters of the Seine, Sarah felt the chill of the wind and crossed her arms over her chest, the hairs on her arms raised in goose bumps. Benjamin, seated next to her on the row of green plastic chairs, reached his arm around her and pulled her close. And, whether it was the wine or the wind or the fact that the boat guide was describing the various points of interest along the river banks giving them an excuse not to talk, Sarah relaxed into the crook of his arm, against his shoulder and felt the strength of his bones and flesh beneath his clothes.

"I rented Pauline's house," Sarah said quietly, after some minutes.

"Excuse? I did not hear you from the wind," said Benjamin withdrawing his arm and turning so he could see her face.

"The mas in Provence. I rented it."

"Brava, Sarah!" he said.

"Do—do you think you might want to visit Mausanne while I'm there?" Before he had a chance to answer, Sarah added, "Perhaps Michel would join you. He told me the house has at least one extra bedroom. And Julie is coming to stay with me as well."

He took his arm from around her shoulder and sat up straight. "Hmm" he said. "I'll have to deliberate." He put his finger to his temple and squeezed his eyes shut tight, as if he were thinking very seriously. After a few moments he opened his eyes and they twinkled at her as he said "I would consider it. Yes, I suppose I will agree to come. That is, if you will promise to cook for me!"

"You'll be my guinea pig."

"What does this mean—your pig?"

"It means I will experiment with you," Sarah said.

"Sounds intriguing," he said and they both laughed and she burrowed her face in his neck and inhaled the scent of him.

# 21

Benjamin called Sarah every night after their day-long excursion. He told her he was trying to finish grading his students' final exams. They talked about his work and about how she was spending her time. He invited her to stop by his office at the Sorbonne on Friday. She found her way there and knocked on his door. His voice told her to come in with a question mark at the end of his invitation.

When Benjamin saw her standing in the doorway, he stood up from his desk and walked toward her, smiling. She closed the door with her foot and they embraced and kissed and if things had been different they might have fallen onto the old sofa that sat on one side of the small room and made love for the rest of the afternoon. But Sarah was not ready. He held her at arm's length.

"I am so happy you came," he said.

Sarah could only smile and say, "Me too."

His office was light and overlooked a small courtyard. His desk faced the window, barely fitting between the two floor-to-ceiling bookcases. It was covered with papers and printed manuscripts piled on either side of his computer.

Sarah peered out of the window and saw a number of students with their books—seated on the grass and at tables. Sarah asked Benjamin whether the law school had a summer session.

"No. These students are preparing for the equivalent of your Bar examination."

"High anxiety!"

"No doubt," he replied.

Sarah looked again around his office, studying the bookshelves more closely. She was impressed to see they held copies of textbooks he had either authored or edited. Strains of Mozart—how had she not noticed before?—emanated from a small CD player. It was the Clarinet Concerto in A.

"This is one of my favorite pieces," she said.

"This recording was made by Benny Goodman. A surprise, no? He was fond of the classics."

"You are full of surprises," she said.

"Mais oui!" he grabbed her around the waist and pulled her to him. They kissed again.

"Coffee?" she asked, gently pushing him away.

"Un moment," he said, shaking his head at her in mock disbelief. "OK," he said finally. "Let's go."

On Saturday, Benjamin met Sarah at her apartment. They planned to do some shopping at a market Benjamin often frequented in the 12th arrondissement.

They walked by the different produce vendors with their bins full of shiny purple eggplants, orange and pale green peppers, deep red tomatoes and summer squash the color of sunflowers. Here were the bakers with their fresh loaves and the proprietors of the charcuteries with their cases of artisanal cheeses and cured meats, many topped with plates full of tasty samples. So many different varieties of olives and pates! At the edge of the market were long tables covered with brightly colored fabrics sewn into purses, pencil cases and tote bags. Exotically dressed men wore caftans and woven pillbox hats and, in accented English, told Sarah they hailed from West Africa. Sarah bought souvenirs for Claire, Asya, Sharon and Julie, and purchased small coin purses for each of her staff members at Kelton Hall. Benjamin had gone off to browse while she was shopping at the African bazaar and returned to find Sarah happily examining her treasures.

"They're for everyone at home."

"Of course," he said, and in that instant they both seemed to realize that, in fact, Sarah did not live in Paris.

"I thought we might have a picnic," Benjamin said after they both stood for a few moments without speaking.

"Wonderful!" Sarah said. She was, after all, not going home yet.

They stuffed Sarah's items into a large plastic bag that the African vendor handed to them and returned to the stalls and bought cheeses, cured meats, breads and wine.

"Shall we go to the Luxembourg Gardens?" Benjamin asked Sarah as they left the market and walked to the stoplight on the main thoroughfare, L'Avenue de la République.

"I've never been," said Sarah.

"Then we must go!" He hailed a taxi—since they had so many bundles, he told her.

Benjamin asked the driver to let them out at the Rue de Vaurigard entrance. The sun and the fair weather had drawn crowds of Parisians and visitors alike. Sarah and Benjamin walked toward the Grand Bassin, the Octagonal Lake at the far end of the Gardens. There were children everywhere.

"Marie and I used to take the boys here to sail their toy boats," he said as they walked.

Sarah flinched, as if pricked by a pin. The reality of Benjamin, here before her with his family, felt like a small rebuke.

"In winter it is an altogether different place," he said as they found a bench to sit on and began to open their paper wrapped parcels.

"Is it empty?" asked Sarah, referring to the park but handing him the wine bottle to open.

"Not as empty as one might think," he said. "We have sunny days during the winter and on those days people try to get outside as much as possible. These trees, so elegantly arranged as you see," he said, nodding toward the promenades and arbors, "are in winter without leaves. Their beauty is then sculptural, and the whole park is more spare and quiet and one is given to reflection. I came here often after Marie died to find some peace. As well it helped me to see others enjoying themselves. I knew that, because of our sons, my life would have to go on. I came here, I think, to learn how to do that, for here was life on display."

He looked at Sarah. "I am getting too serious. What I meant to say is that this place has always pulled me to it."

"I can see why," Sarah said, lifting her face to the sun.

Benjamin reached into his pocket for the corkscrew he had brought. They laid out their little feast between them on the bench. Benjamin poured a glass of Beaujolais into a paper cup they'd bought at the market and handed it to Sarah. She drank deeply from the cup and laughed with pleasure.

"What is it? You do like the wine?" he asked.

"Yes, the wine is delicious! Most suitable for our picnic," she said and leaned toward Benjamin to kiss him on the cheek. He caught her face in his hands before she withdrew it and kissed her back with a fervor that made her forget everything but his lips, his mouth, the sweetness of the wine and the heat of the sun overhead.

They decided to take the long walk back to Sarah's apartment after lunch through the chic and crowded sixth and seventh arrondissments. Sarah's large bag of souvenirs thumped by her side as they strolled along the sidewalks and crossed the streets. Benjamin offered to take it but she wanted to carry it herself.

"Oh, Sarah, you must see this! It is superbe!" Benjamin exclaimed, stopping in front of a small doorway above which a sign read "Musée Maillol." "You have not been here before?"

"No," she said.

Benjamin opened the heavy wooden door and they stepped inside to a cool, cavernous interior. A woman at the ticket counter took Sarah's monstrous plastic bag and gave her a claim check in return. Sarah slipped her arm through Benjamin's as they walked through the galleries. On display in the 18th Century building were the bronze sculptures of 20th Century artist, Aristide Maillol, preserved for the public by his model and lover Dina Vierny. She established a foundation, after Maillol's death in a car accident in 1944, for the expressed purpose of gathering his works—those that were not already gracing the Tuileries or owned by other museums—and showing them as a complete collection in a museum dedicated to his genius. In addition to Maillol, the Musée hosted traveling exhibits. On this day, the exhibit was of modern painters from Picasso to Basquiat.

A number of people—a student with a sketchbook, a white-haired couple, and two middle-aged women with their heads together—were in the room at the top of the stairs. In the far corner, Sarah recognized the Picasso, a photo of which was on the poster of the exhibit. It was not a large painting but it stood out from the rest and drew Sarah to it. Benjamin followed her and together they stood in front of "Tête de femme desesperee" in silence.

"Blue and yellow—the colors of the sky and the sun—and yet I have never seen so sad a picture," said Benjamin at last.

"Desesperee," Sarah said. "Hopeless? Is that what it means?"

"If you translate it literally, yes, it means without hope, but the correct translation would be 'desperate'", he said.

"I have felt like that," Sarah said as she focused on the picture of the head of a woman, tilted as though she was looking to heaven for relief from her pain.

"I felt like that before—for a long time," she added.

They viewed the entire exhibit, climbing the stairs to the next floor where the ceilings were low over their heads. When they had seen everything they wished to see, they descended the three floors to the courtyard and breathed in the grassy air of the June afternoon. No one else was outside in the courtyard and when Sarah turned to Benjamin to say something, to ask him about the tiny museum store she had seen on the way in, he drew her to him and kissed her in the courtyard of the Musée Maillol and she kissed him back with a kiss that held in it some sadness as well as the joy of finding one's way out of the dark and away from desperation.

Sarah bought two postcards of the "Tête de femme"—one for Claire and one to keep—and retrieved her bag full of flea market treasures. They walked away from the museum, their free arms entwined.

# 22

"I have begun to think of the future again," Benjamin said, once their espressos arrived. His remark seemed to her to come out of nowhere and yet from a very deep and private place. They were seated at a café, in a glass-enclosed porch that bordered the sidewalk along the Boulevard Raspail. The waiter brought a small plate of macaroons, finding a place for it between the water glasses and espresso cups.

"I think I know what you mean," said Sarah. She looked at him and went on. "I enjoy being with you so much, Benjamin."

He looked out of the window for a minute and grew serious again.

"Have I told you about my idea of owning a vineyard in the Luberon or Les Alpilles?" He asked.

"No," said Sarah, her voice rising in a question.

"It is a common dream among Parisians, professors especially I think, law professors in particular! I began to look at property some months before Marie died even though she was doubtful about the venture."

"Why doubtful?"

"Marie was a practical woman. She kept telling me it would be a lot more work than I thought. She said I would miss the city—the University, my colleagues. She was sure I would grow bored and that in the end it would be a very expensive detour in our lives. Perhaps she was right but I still think about it."

"It was a dream," Sarah said.

"Yes—one I never imagined myself accomplishing alone. Now I think of—I don't know, maybe I'm crazy but I've been thinking of perhaps—one day—"

Sarah slowly nudged the espresso cup away from the edge of the table and put her hands in her lap.

"Perhaps I should not have told you about this. I make things too serious again?" Benjamin lamented. "We are having a good time together. I'm sorry."

"No," said Sarah. "Please. You don't have to apologize."

"All right," Benjamin said, placing some Euros on the table to pay for the espressos.

Benjamin didn't call Sarah for two days. Why had she been so uptight? He had only been sharing his thoughts with her! It was not as though he had invited her to join him in his venture. How self-centered and silly she had acted. She decided to call him. The answering machine picked up. She left a message asking him to call. When he returned her call it was dark. She had been watching "Now Voyager" on television, the Bette Davis film she had seen so many times that even though she couldn't understand much of the dubbed French she knew the story and was engrossed in it when the phone rang.

"Hello?"

"Sarah, it is Benjamin Manet."

"Oh, hello," she said, her heart racing, thinking at once how sweet and formal and unassuming it was for him to use both of his names. She muted the sound of the television.

"I—I wondered if I might come over," he said.

"Now?"

"Yes. I would like to talk with you tonight."

"All right," she said.

He must have been close to the apartment because within five minutes—just long enough to go to the bathroom mirror to brush her hair and put on some lipstick—he rang the bell. She buzzed him up and turned on a few lights.

"Hi," she said, opening her door, the television still on, still muted.

Benjamin put his arms around Sarah and held her tight. They kissed deeply and for a long time. She felt as though she might not be able to stand. She didn't know what to do. She had promised herself they would not make love. Not yet. She was foolish to let him visit this late in the evening, knowing what might happen.

"It's late," she said, separating her body from his. "You must be tired. I can make some coffee."

"I have missed you, Sarah," he said. "Somehow I upset you the other day and I did not mean to do that."

"No, I overreacted."

"It's just that," he went on, "I did not expect to feel this way again—to want to share everything with you—my thoughts, my ideas about things. I have been with others since Marie, but it has not been like this."

"I know," said Sarah. She kissed him lightly, happy that for the moment she had not spoiled things. He kissed her back with the kind of ardor that she knew meant he wanted to make love. He moved his hands from her shoulders to her breasts and she felt desire spread through her body like a slow, warm flood. Still, she pushed him away.

"As much as I want to, I can't."

"But why not? Not ever?" Benjamin noticed the television. "I know this film. It is one of my favorites. I never understood it though—why they didn't try for a life together when they loved each other so." He shrugged, I guess I too cannot have both the moon and the stars…"

"Just not *now*," she said. This was craziness, she thought. She turned away, wanting to cry.

"All right," he said, with a smile, "then I must be patient."

Sarah rang Sylvie, the hostess of the party where Sarah and Benjamin had first met, to say good-bye. She and Benjamin and Sylvie and Jean-Pierre had met for dinner one evening and the two couples had gotten along well.

"You and Jean-Pierre will visit me in Provence, won't you?" Sarah asked. "La lumiere—the light and all?"

"Non, ce n'est pas possible," said Sylvie. "It's impossible, for I will be getting ready for my show the first of September. It is a horrid deadline as I must work the whole summer—August even!"

"I'd hoped you would be able to meet my daughter, Julie. She will be joining me there," Sarah said.

"Alors, Michel told me," said Sylvie. "He said you invited him as well. Where do you plan on sleeping everyone? Not to-gether so soon?" Sylvie laughed.

"I *would* like Michel to meet Julie. There is something about the two of them. I think they would get along. You see, Julie has had a difficult time since her father died. I worry about her."

"This is because you are her mother and why I do not have children. I worry enough about my paintings!"

"If you change your mind—"

"Merci, Sarah," she said. "Oh and Sarah, I wanted to tell you that this is the first time in a long while we have seen Benjamin so happy. Jean-Pierre and I, we think you are the cause of this."

"I am fond of him," Sarah said.

Sylvie laughed. "Yes, well, au revoir Sarah! Let us hear from you."

"Au revoir," said Sarah, hanging up the phone.

Sarah surveyed the apartment again. She had opened and closed all the drawers in the bedroom, the cupboards in the kitchen, gone through the books on the coffee table to make sure she had not slid papers with names and numbers into any of them. Then she checked her watch. It was 8:25 in the morning and at 8:30 Benjamin would arrive to take her to the train. She had learned over the last two weeks that he was never late, never early—just there when he said he would be. How considerate he was; she imagined his law students giving him high marks. He listened, he stated his views with clarity but without insistence, he was on time.

During this month in Paris Sarah had discovered a natural optimism she supposed had been lost. It was Benjamin, of course, but she believed it was more than that. She had begun to climb out of the despair that had become so familiar to her since the onset of David's illness she had failed to recognize it as anything out of the ordinary. It had surrounded her as surely, silently and totally as the fog over the Pacific coast in summer. She'd grown comfortable with the intimacy of despair, the privacy of it—but she knew, unchecked, it would guarantee ruin.

So, in these few weeks, Sarah had discovered a secret ladder, available to her when she needed it. She would step on one rung, then another, miss the sight of her feet, lose her balance, falter, start again. And now, her bags packed, she was prepared for the next stage of this experiment in survival.

The doorbell. The doorway. Benjamin's glasses tilting on his nose after they kissed.

"Do you have everything you need?" Benjamin asked, adjusting his glasses and peering into the living room. He wore navy khaki's, a plaid button down shirt and running shoes. Sarah noticed the ballpoint pen he seemed to carry with him at all times had left a tiny blue stain at the corner of his shirt pocket. It made him seem vulnerable.

"I think so," said Sarah.

"Good," he said. "Well, we'd better get going. You don't want to miss your train."

"Wait," Sarah said.

"What is it?" he asked.

"Hold me." They wrapped their arms around each other and held on with ferocity and longing. "I'm afraid of good-byes," she said after they untangled, as if she needed to explain herself.

"But this only 'a bientôt'—see you soon!" Benjamin said cheerfully. "I will travel to Pauline's as soon as I finish the article on which I am working. It should take me only a few days," he said, kissing her neck.

They lifted her bags, her laptop—which had remained for the most part unused—and purse and she locked the door—leaving the key on the coffee table as Michel had instructed. They squeezed into the elevator and rode down to the ground level in silence.

At this hour on a Sunday, Benjamin was able to zip in and out of traffic, his little car barely pausing as he shifted gears. They arrived at the Gare de Lyon with time to spare. "Voila!" he said. "Here we are."

"Call me when you arrive at the Mas," he said, giving her a quick hug and a kiss for the last time.

"A bientôt," said Sarah, waving to him as he hopped into his car.

# 23

It was early afternoon on Sunday by the time the TGV arrived at Avignon. Sarah had fallen asleep and was shaken awake by a kind, grandmotherly woman whom she had met when she first got on the train. "Madame," the older woman said gently, "we arrive at Avignon."

"Avignon?" Sarah pushed her hair back with her hand and opened her eyes wide. "Oh, merci beaucoup!" She said to the woman who was traveling on to Marseilles to visit her brother.

Sarah sat up, gathered her things and hurried toward the exit where she almost bumped into a young man pulling a suitcase from the luggage rack. She pointed to her two bags and asked him in French if he might help her. He nodded and in moments Sarah and her two heavy bags were deposited on the station platform. The train's engines sounded like they were revving up.

"Vite! Allez!" a mother said to her young son attempting to get him on board before the train started to move.

A man in his seventies, solidly built and neatly dressed with thick white hair combed back from his rugged, sun-browned face searched the small crowd of people who had disembarked. Most were walking to their cars or embracing friends or relatives who had arrived to pick them up. Sarah stood alone, organizing her various bags so she could manage them into the station. The man approached Sarah.

"Pardon, Madame, but you are Madame Coleman?" Monsieur Henri inquired and bowed his head slightly in respectful greeting.

"Why, yes. I mean, mais oui, Monsieur...?"

"Henri Touraine, a votre service." His warm and modest smile revealed a gold tooth. Without another word, M. Henri hoisted a bag in each hand and nodded in the direction of an ancient, dusty red pick-up truck.

It had been quite warm when Sarah had arrived in Avignon, but now, as the roads turned into lanes and the black top into gravel, a slight breeze had come up, stiffened and blew through the open windows, cooling her face. The sun was still high in the sky and huge white clouds promised a change in the dry weather that was typical of Provence in summer. The air smelled of earth and lavender. She and David had never visited the south of France. She vowed, as they drove up a long gravel drive past fields of red poppies on either side, that she would not dwell on what might have been.

"Bonjour Sarah!" Bienvenue a Mas de Lumiere! I am Pauline, and this is Anouk!" Michel's Aunt Pauline called out as she walked from a gated courtyard at the front of the house toward the truck, wrapping a shawl around her thin, tanned shoulders. A large black dog trotted alongside of her. Pauline was a petite, olive- complected woman of a truly uncertain age who wore her dark hair swept away from her face with a tortoise shell headband. Her features were chiseled and delicate with wide-spaced brown eyes.

Sarah climbed out of the truck and inhaled the scent of jasmine. Pauline stretched out her brown arm to shake Sarah's hand. Anouk jumped up in greeting.

"Arrêt, ma petite," she said to Anouk. And then to Sarah, "It is no problem if you do not like dogs."

"Oh, no!" said Sarah. "I'm just not used to dogs. My husband was allergic to them."

Pauline continued, "Henri and I found Anouk last year, she was a stray, a mix of breeds, part Labrador, part shepherd we think. Henri attempted to train her to be a watch-dog but she is rather hopeless in that regard. Alors, Henri will make sure she doesn't bother you."

"She is sweet," said Sarah, petting Anouk whose tail wagged furiously.

Henri was busy shuttling Sarah's things to the edge of the courtyard.

"Enough!" said Pauline. We will get you acquainted with the house and then let you settle down with a cool drink. The travel becomes tiring, n'est-ce pas?"

"Yes, it does," agreed Sarah, as she followed Pauline into the walled courtyard.

The afternoon sun dappled the stones of the courtyard, which led to the house and its blue-painted door. Wisteria vines wound themselves around a wooden trellis and a large, ancient lime tree shaded a glass-topped table surrounded by wicker chairs.

Pauline was efficient and brief as she showed Sarah around. It was a two-hundred-year-old house, built entirely with local stone—colored a kind of gray, washed white in places from the wind, the rain and the hot sun. Wooden shutters, painted the same peacock blue as the front door, framed the windows and were, Sarah learned, not only for decoration but to protect the rooms from the extremes of weather. Grape leaf ivy climbed the stone walls, obscuring them completely in places.

They walked through an arched entry that led to the main floor. This level consisted of a living room with a large stone fireplace at the far end and a simple dining area that opened onto the kitchen. The kitchen itself was small but well equipped with a black enamel gas cooking stove. There were beautiful antique sideboards and armoires filled with copper pans and porcelain baking dishes. The counters of hand-made tile reminded Sarah of her kitchen in Woodland Hills; everyday dishes were stacked on shelves that hung over a large double sink. The low ceilings were crossed with heavy wooden beams and the whitewashed walls were hung with drawings and prints.

Sarah had spoken with Pauline twice before their meeting thus Sarah knew Pauline was to depart the next day for the tiny Greek island of Monemvasia, just off the Peloponnese, where she spent a month each summer. Pauline had informed her that Henri, her caretaker and friend, would remain on the property in his own small cottage. As they climbed a wooden staircase Pauline apologized for the disarray in her bedroom insisting Sarah occupy it once she was gone.

"I will have these clothes," gesturing to those currently piled on the bed, "packed up by the time I am to leave in the morning! I would have left this weekend," she explained, "but I like to meet my guests if possible, to acquaint them with the house myself."

Pauline went on to say how each bedroom upstairs had a bathroom 'en suite'. Sarah and her guests should be careful not to run both showers at the same time if either was to have sufficient water pressure. Sarah had told Pauline when she had spoken to her on the phone that Julie would be joining her. She had added that Michel might be coming down at some point as well with a friend of his, Benjamin Manet.

"Michel loves Mas de Lumiere," Pauline had said. "Naturellement, as it will belong to him one day."

They walked out of Pauline's bedroom together and stood on the second floor landing. "Since I am to leave in the morning, I have been too busy to think of dinner and the necessary preparations. We are fortunate that one very nice restaurant in Mausanne remains open on Sunday evenings. We can go there together if you like, unless you are too tired?"

"It has been a long day," said Sarah.

"Why don't you rest a bit," Pauline said, gesturing toward the second bedroom across the hall. "Tomorrow, Henri will help you move your things to my room once it has been cleaned and made up with fresh linens. I have a girl who comes in twice a week to help out. She will continue—Mondays and Thursdays at noon—while I am gone."

"Merci, Pauline," said Sarah.

"Alors, we will have a glass of champagne on the terrace at seven. You may decide about dinner then. In the mean time, Henri will bring you an iced coffee."

"You are very kind."

"De rien," said Pauline, waving away the compliment with her hand as she turned toward her room.

Sarah watched Henri slowly make his way up the staircase as he balanced a tray with the iced coffee and a bowl of fresh fruit.

"Merci, Henri," said Sarah leading him into the bedroom. "Here?" Sarah suggested, pointing to a small writing table in the corner. Henri placed the tray on it.

"You have all you need, Madame?"

"Yes, thank you," answered Sarah.

J.S. Tyndall

At seven, Sarah came down the stairs, refreshed from a bath and dressed in a long skirt with heeled sandals.

Pauline was not yet downstairs. The quiet was broken only by the sounds of bees and crickets as Sarah stepped into the courtyard. The sun was low in the sky and cast long shadows on the table. A cool breeze, scented with lavender and orange blossoms blew Sarah's hair away from her face.

This time it was Pauline who appeared with a tray. She, too, had dressed for the occasion and, perhaps in anticipation of her upcoming journey, wore an exquisite Byzantine-style gold necklace with a turquoise silk blouse over a pair of white cotton pants.

I hope to age that gracefully, Sarah thought as she watched Pauline place the tray on the table.

Pauline lifted the Champagne glasses, gave one to Sarah, and made a toast. "Aux voyages des femmes!" The Champagne sparkled in Sarah's mouth.

"Yes," said Sarah. "To the journeys of women."

The restaurant, Le Lapin, in Mausanne-les-Alpilles, had twelve tables set in the dining room, all but one occupied. There were several people waiting at a small wine bar. The owner, Jacques Boulez, a short man with dark hair, greeted Pauline warmly. Pauline nodded politely to several of the diners in the room as they followed Boulez to their table.

Both the waiter Girard, the owner's nephew, and Pauline encouraged Sarah to order the rabbit as a main course. Sarah had never tried rabbit, resisting the assurances of "it tastes like chicken" that invariably accompanied the suggestion. Sarah agreed, but ordered an appetizer that appealed to her in case the rabbit was inedible. Pauline chose a Côtes du Rhone.

The waiter brought them some warm bread with cold un-salted butter and poured the wine into oversized glasses. Sarah looked across the table at Pauline and smiled.

"I feel lucky to be here," Sarah said, truly feeling awkward in her attempt at conversation.

"When will your daughter be joining you?" asked Pau-line. Pauline's brown eyes were clear and fringed with short, dark lashes.

"In a week," said Sarah. "She has never been to France," she added.

"She speaks no French?"

"No, she doesn't. But I do. I mean I can get by reasonably well."

"Of course," said Pauline.

Girard appeared with their appetizers—a sauté of wild mushrooms served on thinly sliced toasted baguettes. The small plates gave off a savory aroma as he set them down. "Merci, Girard," Pauline said.

"This is delicious," said Sarah. I think there is a touch of sherry, and a bit of cream—shallots and parsley. So simple."

Pauline studied Sarah for a moment, her thin eyebrows arching. "Hmm," she said. You like to cook?"

"I do," said Sarah brightly, hoping at last to have found a topic they could discuss. "In fact I have enrolled in a cooking school—École de Provence—here in Mausanne. The classes be-gin next week."

"Ah, Francoise Ullman. It is her school. She is a friend of Jacques—we must tell him."

Jacques stopped at their table as they finished their ap-petizer.

"You like this dish, Mesdames?"

"Si, beaucoup, Jacques. Alors, my visitor from California, Madame Sarah Coleman will be staying at the mas for a month. She has enrolled in Francoise's école. All these Americans who fancy themselves gourmet cooks!" Pauline sniffed. "They flock to Provence as if a week or two with Francoise will turn them into chefs de cuisine. Mme. Coleman has come to Mausanne for this reason."

"It is only part of the reason," Sarah quickly added. "My husband and I always wanted to visit Provence."

"I am glad you come now, Madame," he said graciously.

"Please, call me Sarah."

"You will enjoy the classes with Francoise. She is an excellent teacher and a very good friend."

"I'm looking forward to them," said Sarah.

Once the owner left, Pauline said, "I am fond of Jacques and feel quite at home at Le Lapin. Do not be afraid to come here by yourself. I know how it is to be alone in a restaurant."

Dinner arrived. It was a ragout of rabbit in red wine and herbs served over wide hand-made noodles. Sarah was delighted with the experiment and thanked Pauline for encouraging her to try something new.

"Otherwise," said Pauline cryptically, "what is the point?"

# 24

By the time Sarah awoke the next morning Pauline was gone. They had bid each other good night when they returned from dinner but Sarah assumed they would see each other once more the following day.

A note from Henri, written in awkward letters told her he had taken Madame. He added that there was coffee and brioche in the kitchen and that he would return in the afternoon. The house was silent except for the trill of quail.

Sarah took her breakfast outside on the back terrace, which overlooked Pauline's cherry orchard. The coffee was dark and rich. She spread the brioche with preserves labeled 'Les Cerises de Mas de Lumiere'. It was difficult to envision Pauline putting up preserves from the ripened fruit of these trees, but then Pauline was a mystery. Sarah's thoughts drifted over the tops of the trees to the hills dotted with other houses in the distance. Benjamin would be arriving soon. She could not imagine a more romantic spot. Because of the length of her stay in France—because it was both long enough to meet him and become involved but so compressed in time due to the pulls of the real world—every event and decision seemed telescoped and of a more urgent nature. Then there was Julie. Sarah would call her tonight to tell her how lovely the house, in fact, was.

Once Sarah had finished breakfast, she brought in the tray and washed the dishes by hand. Then she climbed the stairs to get dressed. Before going into her temporary quarters, she pushed open the door to Pauline's bedroom and peeked inside.

The master bedroom overlooked the rear of the house and thus had the same view as the back terrace though from a higher vantage point. A window seat ran along the far wall of the bedroom where one could sit and gaze past the cherry orchard all the way to the chalky hills – Les Alpilles. Much of the land in the nearer distance was planted in grapes, row after row, with the balance left either to tall grasses or olive trees with their silvery leaves.

Sarah thought of Benjamin and the prospect of their nights together—perhaps here in this room. How would it work? How would they find one another? The simple and private loneliness that had been Sarah's reality since David's death was about to be tested, even set aside. Much as she wished for the connection with Benjamin to hold, she feared losing the intimate cloak of grief that had protected her heart.

ॐ∽

Sarah left the house to walk to the village of Mausanne-les-Alpilles. It was mid-morning. She wanted to explore her new surroundings and she knew from experience that getting out for a walk usually lifted her spirits and distracted her from worry. The village was less than a mile from the house along a narrow road.

Sarah turned the corner of the street that led to the center of Mausanne and stopped as she came to the main intersection. On the right was a small café with tables outside and a young waitress bustling back and forth taking orders. Across the street was a gathering place filled with more tables—presumably an extension of the café—a large fountain and a very old church. She continued further down the main road and soon discovered a bakery with patrons lined up ordering their breads and desserts for the day. The bakery smelled of yeast, herbs, butter and chocolate. She would return to the bakery before going home but Sarah's immediate mission was to find the cooking school in which she had enrolled.

The school was located in a wholesale gourmet- foods outlet two blocks off the main road. Jars of black olive tapenade, tomato sauce and eggplant caviar were arranged on tables and in gift baskets. Sarah asked the young man at the register after Francoise, the cooking teacher. Mme. Ullman was not in today, he replied, but he could confirm Sarah's enrollment in the cooking school. Here she was, he said, indicating her name on a list. A class on sauces of all kinds—reductions and demi-glaces would begin at eleven on Monday morning. The group would meet twice a week for the next three weeks—each week concentrating on a different aspect of Provençal cuisine.

Sarah thanked the young man and returned to the village. She dropped into a chair at the Café Centre she had walked by earlier. The same busy waitress appeared and Sarah ordered a café au lait, speaking to the girl in French, telling her she had come to live in Mausanne for a month, and that she would be renting a house. The waitress smiled politely and nodded her head as she cleared the ashtray and dirty cups from Sarah's table.

For a while Sarah watched people come and go. She felt as though she were the only woman in the village without a purpose. In order to shake the feeling of panic she felt, she paid for the coffee, got up, and walked to the end of the shop-lined village street before it became a country road once again. There was a produce market at the very end where Sarah stopped and bought a few things, then she retraced her steps buying milk, cheese, and wine along the way. She picked up a baguette and a small quiche at the bakery she had passed earlier, planning to eat the quiche for lunch. It was still hours before she could call Julie in Los Angeles.

Preoccupied, and not familiar with the route, Sarah passed the lane that led to the house and had to turn back to find it. She carried Pauline's straw shopping basket with leather handles. It was heavy and the sun was hot on her neck as she walked toward the house. She wondered, just for a minute, what she was doing alone in the French countryside and tried hard not to cry as she kept on.

When the sun had finally set on what had seemed like a very long day, Sarah dialed Claire's apartment using the calling card she bought in Paris. She needed to 'refill' it as it was running low but she could only do that online and she had forgotten to ask Pauline if they had any kind of Internet access at the mas.

"Hello?" It was Julie.

"Hi, sweetie, it's Mom."

"Oh, hi," said Julie.

Sarah hoped for as little drama as possible. She hoped for good news. "How are you? I'm so glad you answered because I wanted to tell you about this place. It's beautiful! I can't wait until you see it."

"I'm glad you're having fun," said Julie.

"Actually, I'm a bit at loose ends," said Sarah. I'll be glad when you get here. This isn't Paris. I mean it's incredible—this lovely old house and garden but it's very quiet, almost too quiet if you know what I mean."

"Yeah, well, just be glad you aren't here."

"Why?" asked Sarah.

"Just that Grandma, the way she is, it's so depressing. She's better I think—her cold or whatever. Asya keeps trying to cook for me. I don't know what I'm doing here. And I really don't know what coming to France is going to accomplish—I mean in the scheme of things."

"So Grandma is all right?" Sarah wanted to confirm this one positive fact.

"Well, yeah, I think so."

"And the Center? Are you still going? Have you seen Tammy or are you staying in Santa Monica?"

"I told you the last time, Mom. I volunteer in Santa Monica and I see Tammy in the Valley once a week. It helps. It's all good but it doesn't fix my life."

"I thought you were feeling more optimistic," Sarah said.

"I guess. But are a lot of things I'd rather do than live at my grandmother's apartment with her crazy Bulgarian caregiver who fries everything in gobs of oil and thinks I'm too skinny!"

"Look, Julie, you have to put this into perspective—"

"Perspective! That's easy for you to say. You've got a job to go back to! You've got a life! What do I have?" Julie's voice had gotten increasingly loud.

"You have a life too. A sweet life—remember?"

"Yeah," said Julie, quieter now.

"I just wanted to let you know how much I'm looking forward to your visit here." Sarah steadied her voice. "You can stay as long as you like. We'll figure out what happens next together."

"OK," said Julie as though she didn't have the energy to continue the argument. "Do you want to talk to Asya? She's here."

"Sure," Sarah said. "Put her on."

The next morning after breakfast Sarah joined Henri to work in the garden. He had started tomatoes and peppers before Sarah arrived and the first fruits were ripening. Like all good cooks, Sarah preferred to use fresh herbs. In the afternoon she and Henri shopped for full leaf lemon thyme, purple basil, oregano and tarragon—all in pots. It was too late in the season for seeds. Rosemary bushes spread their pungent needles throughout the property, thus no need to buy more.

Sarah heated up some soup for herself that evening and ate watching the news on TV. She felt as though life was on hold until Benjamin's arrival, and Julie's after that. She would spend the week preparing for them. Benjamin had called while she was slicing bread to have with the soup and had asked if Friday would be all right. He would be finished with his work by then and take an early train. Of course, she said.

Sarah spent the next few days settling in to the rhythm of life at Mas de Lumiere. She moved into Pauline's bedroom and put all her clothes away and piled her books on the nightstand. She had tried her laptop but was unable to access the Internet so packed it away in the closet. There was a computer at the tourist bureau in Mausanne where she would be able to buy more time on her phone card. It was difficult to operate, though, with its French keyboard and weak connection and as a result sent fewer e-mails, did only what she had to do online, and wrote more postcards. She had bought a spiral notebook in Paris to use for notes in the class she intended to take and it lay on a writing table with a packet of postcards and pens. Sarah's mother, Claire, had loved to send and receive postcards and although she no longer traveled and could not read the ones sent to her, she would display them in the corners of the mirror over the dresser in her bedroom. Sarah meant to ask Asya if they had received the ones she sent from Paris yet and whether Asya had read them to Claire.

So Sarah organized her things at the house, drank coffee in the mornings on the terrace, and worked with Henri in the garden. She would walk into town to the post office to buy stamps and mail her postcards, then stop for a café crème or a light lunch and wander through the shops and markets. Between the work in the garden and the walks into town, by Friday Sarah had color from the sun and was anticipating Benjamin's arrival with a combination of excitement and anxiety.

# 25

When Henri had gone to pick up Benjamin at the four o'clock train, Sarah had only to brush her hair and put on a bit of makeup and then decide which of two or three outfits to wear. She had already bathed and sprayed her best cologne behind her ears and neck. She had less than an hour before they arrived but she didn't want to get dressed just yet. Rather, she tied a taupe colored satin robe around her waist—an extravagant purchase she had made one day at a small lingerie shop off the Boulevard St. Germain—and unfolded herself on the large bed, pillows plumped up and the spread smoothed as though it had been freshly ironed.

Sarah thought about her preparations. There was a Bandol rose chilling in the refrigerator, a baguette from her morning bakery run, and some pate and cornichons for an appetizer. She had considered preparing a special meal for Benjamin's first night but decided against it.

Sarah closed her eyes. The next thing she heard was the sound of Henri's truck rumbling over the gravel driveway. She sat up, realizing she'd fallen asleep, and listened to the metallic sound of a door slam shut. She hurried to the bathroom and brushed her freshly washed and dried hair until it gleamed in the sunlight that streamed in the small, high window. Since this bedroom faced the back of the house, Sarah could not see Benjamin, who had already entered the courtyard and, not finding Sarah on the main floor or outside on the terrace, was already climbing the stairs.

Sarah was coming out of the bathroom to choose between the jeans and oversized peasant blouse that fell open at the neck or the pencil thin cotton print skirt to be worn with a deep v-neck brown knit top when Benjamin appeared at the open doorway. They each stopped short and stared at the other, then they both began to laugh—hearty, wonderful laughter. Benjamin put down the leather duffle bag he carried and said, "Hello, Sarah."

Sarah's eyes sparkled, her face glowing with pleasure and anticipation, and she flew—it felt like flight—into his arms. She kissed his warm face and neck and held him close, pressing all of her body into his. This was happiness: this moment out of time, this promise of delight. Benjamin again laughed out loud and held her at arm's length. He traced with his right hand the smooth skin of her cheeks, the crinkles at the corners of her eyes, the soft lobes of her ears and kissed her deeply until Sarah felt she would lose her balance completely.

"My darling Sarah," he said.

"Yes?"

"Do you know how I have wanted this? How I have wanted you? Ever since the evening we met at Sylvie and Jean-Pierre's. Ever since then."

"Me too," said Sarah. "And to think I almost left the party before we had a chance to talk!"

"What is the expression? It was meant to be?" asked Benjamin, kissing her on the neck, breathing in her fragrance, her clean skin, her perfume smelling of roses and vanilla. "Sarah, let me bring up the rest of my things. I have left poor Henri downstairs without instruction."

"I have wine chilling and a few things to nibble. Let me go down with you. I'll just be a minute." She began to untie her robe and was about to remove it and put on her clothes when she was overcome with shyness and with the intimacy of the moment. She took her jeans and top into the bathroom. Then she called out to ask, "What about Henri? What will he think of us staying together in the same room?"

"Sarah," Benjamin smiled, "This is France! Let me worry about Henri. He understands we are grown people. Why would I bother to travel all the way from Paris if not to sleep with such a beautiful woman? He would think it crazy if I had anything less in mind!"

Sarah, walked out of the bathroom, raised her eyebrows and smiled back at him. Then she followed Benjamin down the wooden staircase to retrieve two wineglasses and a tray and the small repast that would serve as a prelude to their first full evening together, the first time since losing David that she would not have to wake alone.

Sarah and Benjamin lay together but were not entwined. They lay in the master bedroom of Mas de Lumiere. It was night, the middle of it or nearly morning, as she woke and sensed Benjamin next to her. She lay on her back and watched the moonlight seep through the uncovered corners of the windows, uncovered by the drapes they had pulled shut wondering if they even needed to pull the drapes when all the windows overlooked was the cherry orchard and the distant hills. But they did pull them closed, if only to create in their own minds a more private retreat for their first night of lovemaking, of sleeping in the same bed.

Tears welled in Sarah's eyes. She hoped Benjamin would not wake, would not notice the tears his presence had precipitated. She had not been able to free herself completely earlier that night. Even with the wine, even with his sweet kisses, his lingering kisses, his attempt to kiss her there and there, his appreciation of her body and her appreciation of his. She had to reassure herself that this was only a start, a beginning. They needed to develop the trust and the knowledge—the knowledge of each other's bodies and wants and preferences and desires—of lovers. It was his own passion that had found release with her permission, with her urging him that it was all right.

The tears ran down her face and she got up from the bed naked and walked into the bathroom. She closed the door and went to the tiny window, opening it further to let in fresh air, the fresh night air and found not the moon (it must have been over the orchard, it must have been beautiful) but the moon's light. And she began to cry for herself and for David and for Benjamin and the wife he had lost. She sat on the edge of the toilet and cried, her face in her hands. It had been so long since she'd made love.

When the brilliant morning light spilled through the corners of the windows, Benjamin turned toward Sarah and pushed the hair from her still closed eyes and kissed her forehead. She opened her eyes and pulled him to her. The skin on his cheeks was rough with a day's growth of beard and he offered to get up and shave and she offered to brush her teeth and they laughed again at how conventional they were.

"I'll go first," said Sarah.

"I'll open these drapes," Benjamin said as they got up from their respective sides of the bed and met at the end of the bed and wrapped their arms around each other. Sarah walked with him to the window and they drew open the drapes together and watched the early morning mist rise up from the grass and the cherry trees and the mist on the hills clearing to what was sure to be a warm, sunny June day.

They laughed as they looked at the view and held each other and then reluctantly let go. "Shall I bring up some coffee?" Benjamin asked.

"Mais oui! And some bread and preserves! We'll have breakfast in bed—how delicious," said Sarah. "Henri usually has a small breakfast prepared in the morning. He leaves it for me before going off to do his chores."

"I will make it myself if he has not already done so," said Benjamin as he pulled on his pants over his shorts and left the room barefoot with one shirt sleeve on and one hanging behind him.

The breakfast tray, with its basket and plates, lay on the writing table. Coffee cups and saucers perched on the night-stands on either side of the bed. And this time, with the windows bare of curtains, with the sunlight streaming into the room and warming their bodies, Sarah and Benjamin explored each other slowly, gently, with the urgency and patience that only a certain age and some personal sorrow can bring to lovemaking. This time, Sarah listened when Benjamin told her to relax, to let him please her. She did as she was told and allowed this man with the wiry body and hair and glasses to make love to her, to hold her breasts in his hands and let him massage and taste her until she had no choice but to give up the part of her that she had been holding back—not wanting to hold it back—and release herself to him in pure joy.

# 26

The weekend passed quickly. It was already Sunday. Benjamin would leave the following morning and Sarah would begin classes at the cooking school. Julie was due to arrive on Tuesday. This was the last evening Sarah and Benjamin would have the house entirely to themselves. Rather than going out they prepared a simple meal together that they had shopped for earlier in the day.

They had had bought candles that morning, along with the rest of their groceries, simple white utility candles normally used for emergencies. The shops in Mausanne catered to many of life's pleasures, which in France are found under the category of basic necessities. Marvelous cheeses and cured meats—hams and salamis—were sold in one shop that also offered not only the uncomplicated wines of the region but the famous, complex and very expensive Bordeaux and Burgundies. Together they decided on a roast chicken for dinner with the last of the late asparagus. They bought tiny Nicoise olives and slices of salami to have as an appetizer with more of the bread sold at their favorite bakery. For dessert they agreed that cherries from the orchard would be just right.

They felt as easy and comfortable together in the kitchen as they did in the shops, on walks around the small and charming Provençal towns, or in bed. Sarah watched Benjamin rub fresh herbs, sea salt and pepper over the skin of the chicken, stuffing it with garlic and lemon for flavor. It was exactly the way she would have done it. David had enjoyed her cooking but never seemed the least bit interested in how she went about preparing a meal. Benjamin opened a local red table wine and between sips of wine and the cutting and washing of the asparagus and potatoes they managed to end up in each other's arms for kisses that Sarah never wanted to end.

"I am so happy tonight," Benjamin told Sarah, studying her profile, her tawny hair covering her gray-green eyes. They ate outside on the terrace, seated next to each other on the wooden bench so they could both look out over the now dark orchard to the hills and sky. The summer twilight, "l'heure bleue", seemed to last for hours. But when it was gone, Sarah shivered and wondered if it was indeed the chill in the air or a premonition of the solitude to come.

Sarah turned to him, smoothing her napkin in her lap. "I hope this will not be our last night like this," she said.

"How could it be?" he said. "We are just beginning to know each other. And the longer I am with you the happier I am. It is not like anything I have experienced before."

"I feel the same way," said Sarah. "But in two days Julie will be here and things will be different. Sometimes she gets so angry with me! Even though I'm not sure I've done anything to warrant it. Anyhow, I'm concerned about how it will go."

"You forget I have grown children," Benjamin said with a smile.

"You have boys," said Sarah.

"And boys—they are no trouble?" Benjamin laughed and reached for Sarah's hands, taking them in his own, kissing them gently. "You worry too much, you know that?" he said.

"I've been told," she said.

Benjamin left the following morning with promises to return on Friday. They had discussed the possibility of Michel coming along and Sarah encouraged Benjamin to extend the invitation, saying she would phone Michel as well. They parted reluctantly and Sarah hurried to her class on sauces. It was difficult to concentrate on the intricacies of a demi-glace so preoccupied was Sarah with memories of the past weekend and with ambivalence with respect to Julie's imminent arrival. When the teacher called on her to repeat the steps of the process, Sarah hesitated, then apologized, admitting she could not repeat them, that she would need to pay closer attention in the future.

❧⚭

Julie was due to arrive at noon. Henri and Sarah drove Pauline's ancient Citroen to Marseilles—well over an hour's drive from Mausanne. Julie would have already gone through customs in Paris; Sarah knew this. They planned to meet in the baggage area.

Henri and Sarah ran into construction traffic outside the airport. One lane was blocked off and cars stacked up in front of them. Some drivers got out to shake their fists at a situation about which they could do nothing.

"What if she thinks we forgot the time?" asked Sarah nervously, as they sat in traffic that barely moved. She repeated her thought in French, noting the puzzled look on Henri's face.

"We still have time," answered Henri. "But if we are late, she know to wait for us, n'est-ce pas?"

Sarah slumped back in her seat, dwelling on all the things that could possibly go wrong.

Sarah popped out of the Citroen when she spotted Julie sitting on a bench outside of baggage claim. She threaded her way through the crowd of arriving passengers.

"Julie!" Sarah called.

Julie looked up and saw her mother. She stood up and received Sarah's warm hug. Julie was tired and jet-lagged but there was something else, Sarah concluded as they hurried to get everything into the car before one of the armed airport guards made them move away from the loading area.

Sarah had not wanted to hurt Henri's feelings by asking him to ride in the back seat so Sarah spent much of the drive twisted around so she could talk to her daughter.

"You look great, Mom," said Julie, apparently noticing the glowing expression on Sarah's face. "What's going on? Are you having an affair or something?"

Sarah, surprised by the comment, had wanted to tell Julie about Benjamin, but had never found the right time. She concluded it would be better to tell her in person.

"It's the sun and the air and the fantastic food. You'll see! Wait until you've been here a few days."

"Whatever," said Julie.

They decided to stop for a snack at one of the stops along the autoroute which supplied one with food, gas, bathrooms and Internet access among other things. Sarah had a bitter cappuccino, Henri a cup of coffee and a roll, and Julie ordered a chef's salad and a Coke.

"So much for the fantastic food," said Julie, picking out the pieces of ham and cheese in her salad and leaving the rest.

"These are like the old Howard Johnson's back in the States," said Sarah.

"Like what?" asked Julie, drinking her Coke.

"Mother would tell me about them. Never mind. Anyhow you cannot possible judge French cuisine from these places."

"I know, Mom, I'm not completely stupid."

Henri read a newspaper until it was time to leave. Sarah asked Julie a few questions about her trip and for news about Claire but conversation was awkward. For one thing, Sarah did not want to ignore Henri. So, they stayed just long enough to eat and use the restrooms. Sarah was anxious to get back to the Mas.

Even though Sarah excitedly pointed out the poppy fields and the road bordered by plane trees that led to Mas de Lumiere, Julie seemed to want nothing more than go up to her room for a nap. "Go ahead," said Sarah. I'll wake you in a couple of hours. I'm making dinner for us tonight."

"OK, Mom," Julie said as she trudged upstairs, following Henri to the guest room, seemingly oblivious to the charms of the house. Sarah sighed and went into the kitchen to begin preparations for a simple pasta with zucchini and tomatoes from the garden.

"Anyway," Julie said putting her cup down, "I don't know what to do about the apartment in New York. I hate to give it up."

"When do you need to let them know?" Sarah asked, disappointed that Julie had not commented about the pasta, which had turned out well, or the wine or anything at all about Mas de Lumiere. They sat at the dining table drinking their coffee. Sarah broke one of the thin chocolate-dipped cookies from the patisserie in Mausanne into pieces, then ate it slowly, one piece at a time.

"I should let them know as soon as possible—August at the latest. The girl I sublet my room to leaves after Labor Day."

"Are you thinking of staying in L.A?"

"I don't know," said Julie. "I don't know anything anymore."

"I think you should try and set these decisions aside for a while," Sarah said. "At least for a week, you know?"

"Yeah," said Julie. "Here I am. In France. I should make the most of it, right?"

"Right," said Sarah. "Now come help me with the dishes."

"On my first night?"

"Absolutely!" said Sarah with a laugh.

Later in the evening, Benjamin called to confirm that he would be coming back to Mausanne on Friday.

"I'm glad," Sarah said, her heart beating hard.

"How is Julie?" he asked.

"A bit irritable," said Sarah.

"Give her a few days," he said. "About Michel, he wants to come. You didn't have a chance to call him?"

"Oh God, I forgot."

"It's not a problem. Are you sure you can manage everyone?"

"This is practically Michel's house. As long as you will help me—I mean you will help me won't you, with cooking and all? Julie is hopeless in the kitchen."

"Of course, my darling," he said.

Julie walked into the living room while Sarah was talking on the phone. She looked at her mother questioningly. Sarah nodded her head and held up a finger as if to say she would explain once she got off. Julie plopped down on the sofa next to Sarah and picked up a magazine.

"Julie just came down," Sarah said.

"You need to go then?" Benjamin asked.

"Yes," said Sarah. "Shall I ask Henri to pick you up on Friday?"

"No, we will rent a car. We should be there by six, maybe a little later."

"Good," said Sarah, wishing Friday was already here. "See you then."

"So? Who was that? Wait—let me guess. It was your new boyfriend, right?"

"He's not my boyfriend, but we *have* been spending time together," said Sarah. "He is a—a special friend."

"Well this is just great," said Julie. "Why did you even want me to come here? You sounded so lonely!"

"I missed you! And I thought this trip would be a good thing for us. One has nothing to do with the other."

Julie picked up the magazine again and flipped through the pages with a sulky look on her face. Sarah turned around on the sofa to face Julie and sat cross-legged against the corner of it.

"Julie. We need to talk."

Julie didn't look up.

"His name is Benjamin," Sarah went on, "and I met him through the people who owned the apartment in Paris. In fact, the son of the owners is a good friend of Benjamin. His name is Michel and he's darling—handsome and smart. They both teach at the Sorbonne—Benjamin is a law teacher and Michel teaches history. It's Michel's aunt who owns this place and both men are coming to visit this weekend."

"Both of them? I don't believe it."

"Why?" It could be very nice—fun, in fact, for us to have company."

"But I just *got* here! I thought we were going to have some time alone together. I thought that's what you wanted."

"I do. And we will have time together. And you will have time on your own too when I take my class on Thursday."

"That's *right*. I forgot about your cooking class. I don't know why I came. I have to figure out my life. It seems you've already figured out yours."

"I wish," Sarah said, looking at Julie. Then she added, "You seem pretty angry."

"Angry? Why would I be angry?" Julie said, getting up. "Forget it. I'm going upstairs. By the way, where are all these people going to sleep? Do I have to give up my room for what's his name?"

"Michel? No—of course not. He'll sleep on the sofa—here," Sarah pointed to where she was still seated.

"I thought this place *belonged* to him—or his aunt or something," Julie said as she walked toward the staircase.

"It does, but he's very gracious, Julie. He'll happily sleep on the sofa." Julie did not respond or look back at her mother. Rather, she climbed the stairs to her room.

# 27

The next morning Sarah stopped at the door to Julie's room. It was closed and she didn't hear any sounds. There had been a light on in the room when Sarah went to bed. It was a sunny, warm day and Sarah was determined to cheer up her daughter and make things work. She had told Henri days ago that it wasn't necessary to wait on her in the morning. She brewed the coffee and warmed two brioches in the toaster oven. She took out the butter and the preserves and prepared a tray to take outside on the terrace. Sarah herself had slept in and it was after nine when she walked back upstairs to wake Julie.

Julie groaned when Sarah came in to sit down on the side of her bed. She was lying on her stomach. Sarah pulled the thick dark strands of hair away from Julie's face and bent down to give her a kiss.

"I've made us breakfast. Come on. This is going to be a good day—your first full day at Mas de Lumiere."

Julie groaned again and turned over. Her large, brown eyes opened reluctantly.

"Mas de what?"

"Mas de Lumiere—House of Light. Pauline—that's the owner—must have named it. A lot of people name their homes around here. You'll see when we go for a walk."

"Oh God, not one of your walks," Julie said, a smile creeping across her face. "Is that what you've planned for us today?"

"No," Sarah said, responding to the tease in Julie's voice. "I thought we'd go into Saint-Remy for lunch and to shop around.

It's a lovely town. But you have to get up first!" Sarah said, rising from the bedside.

"Shopping?" Julie asked, propping herself up on an elbow.

"Right, now get up! I'll see you downstairs."

Sarah was sitting on the terrace when Julie walked out to find her. She wore a cotton jersey top and a pair of pajama bottoms. She was barefoot and her hair fell over her eyes.

"Bonjour, ma fille! Comment ça va?"

"Translation, please?"

"I said, 'Good morning, my daughter. How are you?' I can teach you a little French—just a few phrases to help you get around."

"After coffee. OK, Mom?"


As they walked toward the car, Sarah remembered that the Citroen had a stick shift, something she had not learned to operate well.

"How do you feel about driving in to Saint-Remy?" Sarah asked, even though she had never felt totally comfortable with Julie's driving. "It's a stick shift."

"You'll navigate?" Julie asked.

"I've been there once before. I think I can find the way. In any case, we have a map," Sarah said, pulling one out of her bag.

They made the trip in to Saint-Remy without incident other than making one wrong turn. They circled the town looking for a parking place which they finally found in the public lot next to the Office de Tourisme.

Saint-Remy on a sunny, summer week day was a delight. Not too crowded and made for exploring, the center of town encircled an even older center which could only be accessed by narrow walkways along which shops of all kinds stood one after the other. Sarah and Julie stopped in a gourmet store that sold exotic spices and herbs from all over the world. Sarah bought several curries, measured out and spooned into cellophane sacks at what she thought were very reasonable prices. They browsed in a home and linen shop and Sarah bought some finely woven and colorful towels and napkins in bright colors. Finally, they discovered a shop owned by a petite woman who designed her own knitwear. Sarah bought herself a cardigan sweater in a wool and silk weave of purple and blue laced with gold threads. Julie found a knitted camisole that only someone of her age and with her figure could wear and Sarah was glad to purchase it for her. They looked for an outdoor café at which to have lunch. They found the Café des Artistes close to where they had parked near one of the entrances to the town. The two collapsed on rattan chairs at a small table and ordered Cokes with plenty of ice. Sarah was pleased at how the morning had gone and looked forward to the rest of the day.

"Qu'est-ce que vous nous recommendez?" asked Sarah of the waitress, noting she was younger than Julie.

"The salade au chèvre chaud is always nice," she said, in English. Julie looked at Sarah and shook her head.

"It's a salad of baby lettuces," explained Sarah. "The way they make it here is so good. The goat cheese is dipped in olive oil then rolled in bread crumbs and herbs and baked until its warm and almost runny then served on slices of toasted baguette."

"Sounds good," said Julie.

"Deux salades aux chèvre chaud," said Sarah.

"Merci, Madame," said the waitress, collecting the menus and glancing at Julie—from her long dark hair to her skinny jeans—as if to compare herself before going off to the kitchen.

David had taken Julie out to Zuma Beach in L.A. the weekend she turned sixteen so he could teach her to drive a stick shift. Julie had told Sarah how they had driven up and down the length of that enormous parking lot. Julie's birthday was in January so the beach was empty. Father and daughter had evidently argued over Julie's jerky starts and stops and in all the years since then Sarah felt Julie's driving had not improved that much. They were on their way back to the house in Mausanne when Julie slammed on the brakes at a stop sign they had almost rolled past.

"Julie!" cried Sarah. "Watch what you're doing!"

"Will you please chill out, Mom? You're making me crazy." Julie turned right onto an open road, pressed her foot on the gas, revved up the engine and jerked the clutch into second, then third gear. When they began to sail ahead at what was clearly beyond a safe speed limit in Sarah's mind, Sarah cried out again, this time in anger.

"Julie! Slow down! You're scaring me!" Julie slammed on the brake again, downshifting too soon, forcing the car to the right and nearly into the shallow ditch beside the road's narrow shoulder. Julie stopped the car and turned off the ignition. Sarah stared at the fields, some red with wild poppies and others a deep, summer green which would yield lettuces and other crops for the table. She opened her window and a warm breeze fanned her face.

"What was *that* all about?" Sarah asked, still watching the landscape, a circle of crows spiraling down, breaking the air with their loud caws.

"I'm stopping this car," said Julie. "I can't stand the way you try and control every single thing I do. You've become this fearful person. You're turning into your *mother*!"

Sarah's hands were trembling. She recalled Julie's teen age years and felt almost transported back to that period of self-absorption, of calls from pay telephones in the middle of the night and always the threat of self-destruction hovering over Julie's actions if Sarah or David didn't see things her way. Julie was their melodramatic, only child, the one who took up so much space in their lives. Sarah experienced the crushing guilt that always accompanied ambivalent thoughts about her daughter. She hated feeling this way.

"I'm sure I'm like Grandma in some ways," Sarah said, after more than a few deep breaths. "But she wouldn't have come here, to Europe, by herself. If Grandpa Norman had died young, if he had left her like your father did me—".

"Did *us*! He left *us*!" Julie began to cry. "He left me," she sobbed. "*He* wouldn't have let that—that *thing* happen to me in New York. He would have prevented it! It's true. He always made me feel special. Not like you. You worry all the time and criticize everything I do."

"I'm sorry you feel that way, Julie," Sarah said. "I know I can be hard on you, but to say that I criticize everything you do isn't true."

"It *is* true," said Julie. "*You never liked me.*" The words floated in the air between them.

"But I love you, Julie," Sarah said, feeling trapped in the small foreign car, feeling as if she had nowhere to go. "There have been times when I didn't understand you, but there was never a time when I didn't love you."

"Whatever," Julie said.

"You have this way of saying such—such hurtful things. That's what I didn't—don't understand. I should have handled it better and I'm sorry about that. I knew some unhappiness was causing you to say those things," Sarah said. But I couldn't figure out why you were unhappy. It didn't make sense to me."

"I always thought you didn't care," Julie said.

"What?" asked Sarah. "Why would you think that?"

"Daddy always liked me better than you did." Julie began to cry again.

"Oh, darling, I loved you just as much as Daddy. I just didn't know what to do sometimes. Sometimes it seemed like the two of you—"

"The two of us—?"

"Maybe I was jealous! You were his little girl; you could do no wrong in his eyes." Sarah felt embarrassed admitting that she felt this way.

"That's weird, Mom."

Sarah looked at Julie, both of their eyes red and swollen. She began to giggle.

"You're right!" Sarah said. "That is weird."

Neither said anything for a minute; the only sounds were the crows and the rumble of a truck passing by. It slowed down and the driver called out something in French. Sarah waved to him, letting him know they were all right.

"Shall we go home?" asked Sarah.

Julie looked at Sarah. "Look at you, Mom. You're so much more together than I am—so much stronger."

Sarah's eyes filled with tears. "I'm not," she said softly, tears rolling down her cheeks. "I'm just trying to build my life again, from the ground up. I wish I had more to offer you."

"You've given me this trip. You were there for me after the rape. You were strong then." Julie's voice wavered.

"I wish it hadn't happened," said Sarah, regaining her own composure. "It shouldn't have."

"No," said Julie seeming to review the past, looking beyond the fields and crows to where the pale blue sky met the horizon. "I'm sorry I said those things. I didn't mean to hurt you," she said turning back toward Sarah.

"I know you didn't," Sarah said.

Sarah searched her bag for some Kleenex, she always had extra Kleenex around these days. In that respect she was like her mother.

When they returned to Mas de Lumiere the sun was low, its rays slanted so that the house blocked its direct light. The terrace had begun to cool after the heat of the afternoon. Neither Julie nor Sarah commented further on the episode in the car. Rather, they spent a quiet evening watching TV and retired to their rooms at an early hour.

# 28

Benjamin and Michel were to arrive at the Mas at seven. It had been cloudy and humid all day, unusual weather for Provence. Sarah had begun her preparations for dinner hours earlier, partly because she wanted the meal to be perfect and partly to have something to occupy her mind while she waited. She had learned more about reductions in her class this week and had decided to try a sauce using Calvados. Time moved slowly, though, and by the afternoon Sarah was out of things to do.

Finally, after pouring herself a glass of wine and sitting down to watch the news, Sarah heard the sound of car wheels crunching across the gravel driveway. She stood up and walked out of the house. Henri had heard the noise as well, and walked over from his cottage with Anouk bounding in front of him.

Benjamin and Michel got out of the car, a rented Peugot coupe. Henri embraced Michel and beamed—his gold tooth prominent. Anouk jumped up and wagged her tail in greeting.

Julie appeared at the entrance to the courtyard and joined the group. Sarah put an arm around her.

Michel was taller than Sarah remembered as she stood on her toes to kiss him quickly on both cheeks.

"Bonjour, Madame Sarah!" Michel said.

"Bonjour, Michel. I'd like you to meet my daughter, Julie."

"Enchanté," Michel said.

"Hello," Julie said.

Michel looked over at the house and grounds and smiled with satisfaction. "I always like coming back to Mas de Lumiere."

Meanwhile, Benjamin was getting something out of the car. "You brought flowers!" Sarah exclaimed watching him, feeling giddy with pleasure at seeing him again.

"He is much the romantic!" said Michel. "He insisted we stop in Fontvielle to purchase them." Benjamin grinned and nodded, his gaze fixed on Sarah as he handed her a bunch of peonies and roses. Then he turned to Julie.

"Hello, Julie. I am Benjamin, a friend of your mother."

"Hi," said Julie.

Sarah embraced him lightly, kissing him on both cheeks, wishing to kiss his mouth and to be enveloped in his arms. "Merci," she said, glancing down at the flowers in her hands.

"Ah, one more time!" said Michel.

Sarah looked at him with raised eyebrows.

"The traditional Provençal greeting is three kisses—not two," he said.

"C'est vrai," nodded Henri. This is true, he said.

"I'm so glad you're here," Sarah said to Benjamin in a low voice as they walked toward the house together. Benjamin stopped and took her in his arms, embracing her without hesitation or concern for the others.

Benjamin followed Sarah into the kitchen and, with Michel and Henri still bringing in things from the car and Julie having retreated to her room, they kissed and laughed with pleasure. Benjamin began kissing her throat, pulling down her thin jersey to reveal the skin above her breasts.

"We don't have time!" Sarah said.

"I will find it difficult to wait," he said, his glasses tilted on his nose, his blue eyes twinkling.

"Waiting will only make it better," Sarah whispered, her heart beating, wondering at the same time how this would possibly end up.

That night, Michel and Benjamin helped Sarah with dinner while Julie set the table on the terrace overlooking the cherry orchard. Benjamin had purchased two bottles of red wine from the Bouches-du-Rhone region, in which Mausanne was located. They enjoyed the cheeses and pates Sarah had brought from the charcuterie in the village and savored her preparation of grilled pork chops finished with Calvados and served with a delicate timbale of artichokes. Sarah's sun-browned face glowed in the candlelight. Benjamin seated across from Sarah, turned his gaze on her often, although he fully engaged in the animated conversation of the table. Michel had them all laughing with his childhood stories of a city boy spending time in the country. He made fun of himself in a way that was both silly and endearing. Because of this, and also because of the wine, Julie relaxed visibly and began to let down her guard. By the end of the evening the four had come up with myriad plans for the weekend, beginning with a trip to the sea on Saturday. It began to rain lightly, ending the outdoor meal.

"We'll clean up," said Michel, "won't we Julie?" he asked, cocking his head toward Benjamin and Sarah, who were organizing dirty dishes on the kitchen counter.

Julie looked at her mother, almost as if she was seeing her in a different light, seeing her from Michel's perspective.

"Fantastique! Merci, you two," Benjamin said brightly, without waiting to hear anyone's objections. He nudged Sarah out of the kitchen, patting her on her behind.

"You know? I *am* a bit sleepy," she said. "The wine I guess," she added, not looking tired in the least.

Benjamin closed the bedroom door behind them and grabbed Sarah. He lifted her off her feet—something David had never done—and swung her around, kissing her and laughing again.

"You should have seen the look on your face!" he said.

"I felt guilty! Like a teenager in my parents' house."

"No teenager, Sarah, just a beautiful woman who belongs to me tonight."

"Oh, yes." She clung to Benjamin as he peeled down the cotton jersey top, kissing the tops of her breasts. Sarah leaned her head back, wanting to absorb his heat, melting into him and forgetting everything but how their bodies were drawn together as inevitably as the rain coming down.

తౡఆ

"People compare the Calanques to the Norwegian Fjiords," said Michel, their designated tour guide for the afternoon. "Personally, I do not see the similarity, but then I would not trade the village of Cassis for the freezing latitudes of Scandinavia," Michel added as they motored slowly in a rented power boat. He expertly navigated their craft up the narrow waterways, deep blue in the middle, turquoise around the rocky edges. The cliffs reached up toward a cloudless sky, the air washed clear by the rain the night before.

"These cliffs are much smaller and more welcoming than the tall green cliffs leading inland from the North Sea," Michel continued. "And as you can see, they provide many private nooks for sunbathing," he said smiling.

Sarah tried not to stare at couples lazily stretched out on the pale limestone boulders. None of the women wore the tops to their bathing suits and many had abandoned the bottoms as well. It was the sight of male nudity that embarrassed Sarah, a fact about which Michel and Benjamin teased her without mercy.

"You Americans are so uptight about the body!" said Michel.

"We're not uptight! It's just not something we're used to. Right?" said Sarah, looking toward Julie for support.

"It doesn't bother me," said Julie, looking up from beneath her dark lashes. Julie, only three days in Provence, seemed more comfortable than when she had arrived. The contours of her narrow face were softer, and the sun had brought an evenness of color and depth to her complexion.

Sarah looked radiant. She and Benjamin took turns rubbing suntan lotion on to each other's shoulders. Benjamin's were pale in comparison.

"You spend too much time inside, writing your books and articles," she teased.

"You are wrong!" he defended himself. "I ride my bike every weekend. See my arms and legs?" he asked, pointing to the tan lines that indicated where his socks and shirtsleeves had covered his body.

"I see," she said and laughed at this because she was happy.

The trip to the Calanques ended with a dinner of bouillabaisse on the waterfront in Marseilles. The group talked and laughed and consumed a lot of wine. Earlier the Provençal sun had disappeared behind a thick layer of fog, which was followed by a cool breeze. Sarah was cold and reached for the cotton sweater she had tossed on the back of her chair. Benjamin helped her on with it.

The waiter brought a dessert menu and the group ordered coffee.

"I am so full," said Benjamin, pushing his menu aside.

"But you are too thin!" said Sarah. "You *should* have dessert." Benjamin offered to share anything Sarah chose. "Not me," said Sarah, "especially not after seeing all those gorgeous bodies in Cassis!"

"Well *I* shall have le tarte au citron," said Michel. "Would you share it with me, Julie?"

"Sure," she said.

"Deux tartes aux citron," said Benjamin.

Once dessert was consumed and everyone was sipping their coffee Julie cleared her throat and turned to face her mother, clearly affected by the wine and the sun and the new company.

"You know, Mom? I felt sad about leaving the theater, about giving up all the goals I had set out for myself from the time I was in high school."

"Hmm?" Sarah responded, caught off guard, as the conversation had been centered on plans for the next day. Everyone else was quiet.

Michel spoke up first. "I have a friend who is in the drama department at the Sorbonne," he said. "It is very well regarded in Europe."

No one else said anything, so Michel continued. "My friend is proud of the program, and they take some foreign students each year. She also runs a summer acting workshop. I could introduce you to her if you like, Julie." He said her name as if it were spelled with a "zh" at the beginning. Zhu-lee."

Julie smiled at him. "That's very nice of you, Michel."

"What have you been doing, Julie, if not acting?" asked Benjamin. "Your Mother tells me you earned your degree in drama."

"I've been living with my grandmother recently, who is not well, and volunteering in a Women's Center," said Julie. "They provide counseling to women who have been abused in one way or another. And they help them with their legal rights if the victims want to pursue that path."

"Interressant," Benjamin remarked.

"Yes, interesting," said Michel, "but it sounds depressing."

"Not really," said Julie. "It's just that I'm not trained for it and they don't have enough funding for the coming year to pay me and, well, it doesn't feel like the thing I was meant to do. You have to really want to help people—you know? I—I'm too selfish," she said, the words tumbling out of her.

"I don't think it's selfish to pursue something you think will make you happy," Benjamin said, giving Sarah a quick and knowing look. "I imagine," he went on, "that the people who thrive in the career field you describe are driven by their own desires and needs as well. We are all human, Julie, and to be human is to strive for something that makes us happy. You agree? To look for happiness and fulfillment—this is not selfish."

"True!" Michel said before Julie could respond. "I know people who are miserable in their jobs and others who love their work. It is not the work, it is the relationship of the person to the work. It is finding a match, you know? Une harmonie, n'est-ce pas?"

No one spoke for a moment, each one seemingly lost in his or her own thoughts.

"I meant to ask you, Michel," said Benjamin, breaking the reverie, "if you have heard of any properties for sale in the Bouches-du-Rhone—near Mausanne or one of the other villages in the region?"

"No, but Henri is the one we should ask. Henri knows everything that goes on."

"Good. Then I must remember to ask him in the morning."

# 29

"Sarah," said Benjamin, once they were alone. It was late and the sky was midnight blue and filled with stars. They had turned off the lights in the bedroom and left the drapes open. She looked at him.

"Yes?"

"You remember I mentioned to you my dream of owning a vineyard in Provence?

"Of course," replied Sarah.

"It was not the time to discuss it then but now—well, I was thinking that perhaps—I thought maybe *you* might be interested in doing something of the kind—"

"A vineyard? I wouldn't know where to begin," said Sarah.

"You love to cook, yes? You have made such wonderful meals for me—and Michel too—he told me about your dinner for him in Paris. You are taking the classes for cooking and I know you love good wine!"

"What are you saying?" said Sarah, sitting down on the bed, thinking she might know.

"Oof, j'ai pas," said Benjamin, shaking his head. "The food and the wine—they go together," he tried again. "I was thinking you might want to invest with me—".

"*Invest?*" she asked.

"I don't mean invest money," Benjamin said. "I mean an investment of time, of labor, of...of love."

"Come here," she said and patted the space on the bed next to her. He did as she asked and she kneeled on the bed. He closed his eyes and Sarah smoothed the lines on his forehead with her hands and kissed the top of his head. He turned and took Sarah in his arms and held her.

"It is true we have known each other for only a short time," he said in a soft voice, close to her ear. "But I feel this is a chance for both of us."

Sarah pulled away and looked at him. "It does sound wonderful. But I have my job. It's not long before I have to think of getting back. And there is my mother to look after—"

"Someone once said to me," he went on, "when I spoke of writing a particular book, that I 'would never write it younger'. That is all. I am saying—for myself—that if there is something I want to try, I need to stop talking about it and do it!" He banged his hand on the bed for emphasis.

Then, as if he had spent his allotment of emotional energy, he got up and went in the bathroom. Sarah heard the water running in the sink. She called to him over the noise of it.

"Thank you!" said Sarah.

"What? I didn't hear you," he said, coming back into the bedroom with his toothbrush in hand.

"Thank you for including me in your dream," she said softly.


Sunday morning, Sarah slept in. When she came down to breakfast she found Julie and Michel dressed in khaki shorts, T-shirts and neck scarves deliberating over a map spread on the dining room table.

"Where are you off to?" Sarah asked, tying her robe more securely around her waist and walking over to the coffee maker.

"We go for a hike in the Luberon," Michel said. There is a beautiful national park but it is far so we must get an early start."

Julie shrugged and bit into a peach. "It's all his idea," she said.

"Have either of you seen Benjamin?" Sarah asked. "I can't believe I slept so late."

"He has gone to work in the garden with Henri and Anouk," said Michel, folding the map and retrieving a couple of bottles of water from the pantry.

"You should take some things for lunch," said Sarah.

"We will stop in Isle-sur-le-Sorgue," said Michel. "It is on the way and I would like to show Julie this town."

"We're off," said Julie, tossing the peach pit in the garbage and giving her mother a quick kiss goodbye.

"I hope Michel is driving," said Sarah.

"Mom!"

"Do not worry," said Michel. "Oh, and do not wait for us for dinner. We will stop on our way back. It will be late, I expect, before we are home."

"Be careful," Sarah said. "And have fun."


Rather than joining Benjamin in the garden, Sarah walked into the village for some exercise and did some shopping before the Huit a 8—the grocery store she frequented—closed at noon. Church bells chimed in the square near her favorite café as Sarah stopped in for a café creme.

When she returned to the Mas, she found Benjamin sound asleep on the terrace in one of the chaises, his hands still dirty, a book with its pages spread open, face down on his stomach, a baseball cap tilted down over his forehead. Sarah laid her hand on his arm. It was damp with perspiration. He stirred but did not wake. Sarah arranged herself on a chair beside him, feeling a peace she had not known in a long time. She watched him sleep and tried to imagine what her life might be like with Benjamin—life in a place like this. She smiled at the thought of it and closed her eyes so she might see it better.

Sarah and Benjamin lay on the bed in Pauline's bedroom. A small, empty bottle of Champagne stood beside two glasses on the nightstand. The French windows above the window seat were open and a single star pierced the darkening sky. A full, bright moon would rise on the evening—Benjamin's last night in Provence before returning to Paris.

Sarah rolled on her back. She had been lying on her side, close to Benjamin, relaxed in his arms. Their lovemaking had been slow and languorous. Benjamin was a generous lover. As she rolled away from him he propped himself up on one elbow and watched her.

"What are you looking at?" asked Sarah with a smile.

"You," he said. "All of you." He bent down to kiss her ear-lobe, her shoulder. She reached up to touch his mouth with hers and he responded with a warm kiss, a long, lingering kiss. Sarah was aroused all over again but could not expect that at his age he would try and make love again. He covered her body with his own. "Sarah," he said.

"Yes?" she said and she could tell that, yes, it was a possibility. Maybe it was because he was soon to leave or because of the Champagne or because this old house in the country was so damn romantic. She didn't know how or why it was happening and without her having to ask he began to kiss her breasts, the space between her collarbones, her neck until she pulled him down against her and they rocked together with the drapes open and the moon rising and the soft night falling over the landscape.

Sarah cried again this time. The tears rolled down her cheeks and she turned her back to Benjamin for this was too private a moment for her to share. It was Benjamin and it was David and it was losing her other half and it was feeling whole again and the combination of feelings overwhelmed her. It was something she couldn't and didn't want to explain. She also knew it would pass. With Benjamin she allowed herself to let go, to forget herself, forget everything but the moment, and she cried out of gratitude for that as well.

"Sarah," he said softly a little while later, after she had regained her composure.

"Hmmm?" she answered.

"I'm starved!" he said.

Sarah wiped the tears away and turned back toward him, laughing. "You should be!" she said.

"I'll shower and shave and you phone Le Lapin, d'accord?" Benjamin jumped out of bed, turned on the lamp, and walked to the bathroom. Her knees were weak and her eyes were not prepared for the glare of the lamp. She pulled the bedsheet over her head.

"All right!" she said.

Jacques, the owner of Le Lapin, came over to their table to check on their dinners. They had both chosen the delicate salade of baby lettuces with yellow and red miniature tomatoes and Roquefort croutons and a main course of grilled filet of beef. "Delicieuse!" said Sarah, her face glowing.

"You are looking beautiful tonight, Madame," said Jacques.

Sarah blushed as she thanked him and looked at Benjamin as Jacques walked away. Benjamin took her hand. This time she responded by putting her other hand on top of his.

"You do look lovely, my darling, especially lovely," he said. Sarah returned his gaze. His curly salt and pepper hair framed his face; his nose was sunburned from the day on the boat in Cassis. He wore an aqua-colored polo shirt that showed off his blue eyes.

"And you look particularly handsome tonight. We must be good for each other," she said, smiling at him.

"Sarah," he said, his smile disappearing in to a look that was more serious. She released his hand. He took a drink from his water glass as though to prepare himself.

"Sarah," he repeated, "I wondered if you had given my plans, the plans I mentioned about the vineyard, about your staying on in France with me, any more thought."

"Of course I have."

"And, what have you concluded?"

Sarah answered slowly. "Just that, well, it's not really a plan, yet, is it? It's a dream. And it's *your* dream. So if it is only a dream for you, what can it be for me?"

"You say you must return to California," he said. "Have you not noticed the similarities between Provence and California—the wine country especially? I think you would feel comfortable here. The climate seems to agree with you."

"Oh it does," she said. "But I've told you about my job— my career—and my mother in L.A. And then there is Julie."

"I understand about your mother. It is something to consider. But Julie? Who knows where she will end up? She may go back to New York, in which case you are as close to her here as you would be in California. And the career? Is it something you see yourself doing five years from now? Ten? Is it something that fulfills you?"

"I don't know. Other than taking the leave of absence this summer, I never thought about quitting the field. I need an income, you know."

"You are too practical," he said. "I think maybe you are afraid."

"Of course I am! And you? Do you realize what you are asking me to do? Everything is moving so fast."

"Perhaps you are right," Benjamin said, backing away from answering her question directly.

When Sarah and Benjamin returned to Mas de Lumiere the Peugot was in the driveway. Michel and Julie were back. After everyone exchanged news of their day, Benjamin and Michel sat down in the living room to watch a soccer match and Sarah went upstairs. After half an hour or so, Sarah heard a knock on her door.

"Yes?"

"It's me," Julie said.

"Come in," said Sarah.

Julie opened the door and saw her mother wrapped in the taupe satin robe, sitting up in bed with her pad and pen.

"Am I interrupting you?" asked Julie lightly, sitting at the foot of the bed.

"Of course not," said Sarah. Sarah put the pad aside and took her glasses off, folding them carefully and placing them on top of it. All of her movements were careful and quiet.

"I have to tell you what we've decided!" said Julie excitedly.

"We?"

"Michel and me. Mom, I want to go back to Paris with him."

"What do you mean? You barely know him. Have you even—I didn't think—".

"That we were sleeping together? We aren't! We are like brother and sister. I'll be sleeping on his couch and he's going to teach me French. This summer acting workshop he talked about begins in one week. I know because he called his friends. See he knows people who—".

"I remember," said Sarah.

"You don't approve?"

"It's not that," said Sarah. "I thought the two of you might hit it off. When I first met Michel he reminded me of you."

"See? This is all your fault! No really, Mom, you *have* to see! This is a great opportunity. I've been so depressed. I don't think you even noticed," said Julie, casting her eyes downward.

Sarah looked at her daughter and sighed. "You had reason to be depressed, didn't you? But you do seem happier now..."

Julie reached out to Sarah and hugged her. "So, you think it's a good idea? To go with Michel I mean? I'm not sure about the money part."

"Julie, I wish I knew if this was a good idea or not. I'd hate to support something that wasn't," Sarah said. "Look, why don't you see how it goes? How long does the workshop last?"

"Four weeks I think."

"All right. I'll help you pay for the workshop but after that you'll have to have a plan—whether it's graduate school or getting some kind of a job—which, I believe is quite difficult for a U.S. citizen."

"I'll work it out. I promise!" Julie said, and hugged Sarah again. "Thanks Mom!" she added, the words trailing over her shoulder as she ran down to tell Michel the news.

"You're welcome," said Sarah, pushing off the bed pillows and arching her back to relieve the tension in her spine.

When Benjamin came to bed that night Sarah told him about Julie and Michel.

"I think they do it for the adventure and the friendship. It appears they have both been lonely—I know this is true of Michel. It is not difficult to understand?"

"Julie is very confused right now," said Sarah, turning off the light on her side of the bed. "She doesn't know what she wants. Even if Michel is temporarily lonely he's settled. He's a Parisian; his parents live in the city. He's completed his education and is pursuing his life's work. Don't you see? I'm afraid for Julie. I don't want her to get hurt again."

"Again?" Benjamin inquired.

"She has suffered...."

"She is human like the rest of us," he reasoned.

"But too much for a girl as young as she is." Sarah was not responding to Benjamin directly. She was thinking both of David's death and awful experience in New York. She had not yet told Benjamin of the latter because she believed it was not her story to tell.

"Misfortune isn't doled out in equal measure, is it?" he asked rhetorically, as though Sarah were a student of his. "It's the basic inequity of existence."

"Hard to take a philosophical approach when it comes to one's own child," replied Sarah, lowering herself into the bed and pulling the covers under her chin.

"True," Benjamin agreed, turning off his light as well. "Very true."

With so many things on her mind, Sarah did not feel like making love that night, even though it was Benjamin's last night in Provence. Sarah was surprised that he did not insist, and she wondered if he was disappointed in her, if the issue of the vineyard had drawn a line between them, defining the relationship as impermanent. She turned to him and he reached his arm around her, drawing her close. They said nothing more but slept in each other's arms throughout the night.

In the morning Sarah and Benjamin rose early. Benjamin and Michel were to leave on the mid-day train to Paris with Julie in tow and there was much to be done. Sarah had wanted to accompany them to the train but she had her cooking class that morning.

"Merci pour tout," said Michel, giving Sarah the three Provençal kisses.

"You know how much I enjoyed having you here, Michel. I can't believe you are leaving with Julie. You won't let her ride the Métro at night, will you?"

"Horreurs, Madame!" he teased.

Sarah turned to Julie, who had just put her backpack in the trunk. "I'll miss you, girl!" Sarah said, trying to keep it light. "What will I do in this house for the next week—all by myself?" Sarah asked, making a sweeping gesture at the Mas.

"You'll be busy, Mom. Henri and Anouk are nearby. And you'll visit me in Paris before you leave for L.A., right?"

"Of course," Sarah said, reaching her arms out to Julie. They hugged a great big hug—the two tall, lean women looking more like sisters than mother and daughter.

Michel offered to sit in back but Julie insisted he sit in the front with his long legs. Thus, Michel held the seat forward for Julie to squeeze into the back of the coupe. Then he went off to look for Henri. That left Benjamin and Sarah to say good-bye to each other.

"I had a wonderful time," Benjamin said.

"So did I," said Sarah. She began to kiss him as well in the Provençal way. He stopped her and held her at arm's length, then walked her slowly away from the car.

"I love you, Sarah," Benjamin said in a quiet but determined voice. "You know that, don't you?"

Sarah blinked, the sun in her eyes.

"I will call you," he said. They kissed then, this time a lovers' farewell kiss with many questions in it.

"Au revoir!" Benjamin called to her as he jogged to the driver's side. Michel and Henri appeared from the side of the house with Anouk beating them to the car.

"Au revoir, mon ami," said Michel, extending his hand to clasp Henri's mottled one.

"Au revoir, Michel. Au revoir Mademoiselle Julie et Monsieur Benjamin," said Henri.

"Good-bye! Au revoir!" Julie and Benjamin called again from the car as Michel got in and they drove off, causing dust to swirl over the gravel drive. Anouk chased the car while Sarah and Henri waved until the Peugot turned onto the main road that led to Avignon.

# 30

"I have my cooking class at this morning," Sarah said to Henri. They were still standing in the driveway.

"I think you are a good cook already," he said.

Sarah smiled at him. "Merci, Henri, but I should get ready for it anyway." Then she added, "Would you like to have dinner with me tonight? The house will seem very empty now that our visitors are gone."

"Alors, but I cannot, Madame Sarah. I must go to the house of my cousin in Arles. His wife she make a cassoulet for me."

"Well, then, I don't blame you."

Henri looked at Sarah expectantly. "Tomorrow morning, you will work with me in the garden?" He asked.

"Yes," said Sarah. "A bientôt, Henri."

"Have a lovely day, Madame."

Sarah walked inside the house and closed the door. It was still very cool inside. Sarah looked at the clock on the kitchen radio. I must get going, she thought, but her heart was not in it.

That afternoon, after class, she stopped in the tiny village pizzeria in Mausanne for a thin slice of pizza, baked with fresh tomatoes and basil. She ate it with a glass of rose before returning to Mas de Lumiere.

The sun beat on Sarah's face and by the time she got home she was hot and sticky. She climbed the stairs to take a shower and let the warm water beat down on her shoulders and neck and rinse the sweat out of her hair. She thought of Benjamin and the way his body was still limber and firm. The thought stimulated the desire she felt for him and she wanted him and missed him even though he had been gone only a few hours.

She rubbed lotion on her legs and wondered what she would do with herself for the balance of the week with no visits to anticipate and no one to talk to. Just then the phone rang. Perhaps it was Benjamin calling from the train.

"Hello?" Sarah said.

"Sarah, it's Becca."

Sarah's heart sank a little. "Hi!" Sarah said. "How are you? Is everything all right?"

"I'm all right. But Mother's not so great. She's in the hospital."

"What? Are you in L.A.?" asked Sarah, sitting down on the bed.

"No. I spoke with her doctor, she has a new doctor now, a hematologist. Dr. Blooming referred her."

"A hematologist? Why?"

"She's had some difficulty breathing but that's nothing really new. Asya has been giving her inhalation therapy twice a day."

"I know that," said Sarah. "We talked about it the last time we were on the phone."

"Well, anyhow, when Asya took Mom to Dr. Blooming's for her regular appointment she evidently looked quite pale so he sent her over to this other doctor, a young woman, who ran some tests. It turns out her hemoglobin was very low. The doctors told me that can impair breathing by depriving the body of oxygen."

"So what did they do?"

"They put her in Cedars so she could get a blood transfusion. They're doing one today and they'll do one tomorrow."

"A transfusion? Do they know what's causing the problem?"

"They're not sure—possible internal bleeding. Maybe from the Coumadin but they're checking everything out."

Sarah sighed. Internal bleeding. She had hoped Claire would not have to undergo any more procedures. Each one took its toll on her, frail as she had become.

"Are you going to L.A.?" asked Sarah.

"I wasn't planning to. Asya says they're fine. The doctors will release her day after tomorrow. By the time I got there—"

"You'd be able to help Asya get her home. No one is there—no one from the family I mean."

"That's true," said Becca.

"Becca, you'd said you'd take over while I was gone." Sarah's voice grew stronger as she spoke.

"OK. All right. I need to get off the phone then and make my reservations. When are you coming back?"

"I was planning to return next Sunday. Let me think about this. Why don't I call you later? You're your cell with you. I'll get in touch with Asya. It's so early in L.A." Then she thought of something else. "Did Mother have a sitter during the night? She needs to have someone with her in the hospital during the night. Asya can't possibly do it all."

"I think someone was with her last night," said Becca.

"Did you ask for someone?" asked Sarah.

"No," said Becca, "but I think the nursing station did."

Sarah rubbed her forehead with her free hand.

"Sarah?"

"What?"

"I'm sorry," said Becca. "You were counting on me. I should have gone out right away."

"It'll be all right if you go now," said Sarah.

"I will," said Becca.

After Sarah hung up, she contemplated the view overlooking the terrace and the cherry orchard out to the foothills of Les Alpilles. A tractor moved across a field far in the distance, half a world away from Los Angeles. A breeze came in through the open windows. The wind direction must have changed for the breeze was cool and had some scent of the sea about it even though the Mediterranean was an hour away. Sarah kneeled on the window seat, her face against the screen, and breathed in the moist air.

That night Sarah called Asya and found her at the hospital. She told her Becca was on her way. Asya had protested but Sarah was firm. She also called Becca twice more. Becca's flight to L.A. left at six in the evening from Chicago and got in around eight. She would be there in time for the second transfusion, Becca told Sarah.

The next morning Sarah found Henri in the garden. "I cannot work in the garden with you this morning," she said. "My mother is ill and I may need to go home a few days early. I will check into flights."

Sarah, dressed in shorts and a T-shirt, walked into the travel agency—Agences de Voyages—she had passed often. She learned that the cost of changing her ticket was prohibitive. She put a 24-hour hold on one just in case, hoping things would sort themselves out and that she could wait for her scheduled departure on Sunday.

Becca called Tuesday night—morning in L.A.- and gave Sarah a full report. Claire was doing better. The second transfusion was scheduled for mid-morning. The doctors were fairly certain she would be discharged on Wednesday. They had decided to increase her inhalation therapy—a process that delivered enriched oxygen to Claire's lungs—to four times a day. The hematologist in consultation with Dr. Blooming felt these measures would be effective and appropriate considering her overall health. In other words, 'let's make her comfortable'. Sarah knew her mother's condition was deteriorating but Becca assured her it was not critical. Sarah decided to let Becca handle things until she returned to Los Angeles, leaving on Sunday as originally planned.

Sarah called Benjamin to let him know she would be in Paris on Friday. He was very busy, apparently working on a deadline.

"You will stay with me Friday night, n'est-ce pas?" he asked.

"Bien sur," said Sarah. Of course I will. She was already thinking about how she would say good-bye to him.

Sarah spent time with Henri in the garden on Wednesday. Fog had settled over the land early that morning. Sarah, chilled when she left the house, removed her hooded sweatshirt after only a half hour of pulling weeds. It was good hard work and it kept her mind occupied.

Henri and Sarah stood and surveyed their progress.

"You must keep it up," Henri observed in French. "Otherwise it gets away from you."

Sarah nodded. "Henri, I leave here on Friday," she said in French. "After my class I will spend tomorrow packing and making preparations to leave. You understand?"

"I do, Madame Sarah," he said. "What time is your train?"

"It's the morning express to Paris."

"I will drive you," he said. "We must leave by eight."

# 31

During the first hour or so of the train ride to Paris, Sarah let the images of Provence and everything that had happened there drift and settle in her mind like dry leaves. She had been sorry to leave Francoise's cooking class, reflecting on the few techniques she'd learned. She'd really just begun to understand some of the basics of French cooking.

She had telephoned Pauline the night before to thank her and say good-bye. Pauline had been in the middle of a dinner party at her place in Monemvasia.

"You have enjoyed yourself?"

"Yes, Pauline. Very much."

"And your daughter? She came to visit you?"

"She did. I think it was good for her," said Sarah. She decided not to share the details of Julie's current whereabouts, namely on Pauline's nephew's sofa.

"Good. I hope you will come again, Sarah. Next summer perhaps?"

"Perhaps," Sarah had said. She wondered if she would ever return to Mas de Lumiere.

The train ride was uneventful. Sarah carried a book with her. She opened it and tried to concentrate on the story but after a short time her eyes closed and she slept as the train sped through green fields on its way to the gray industrial zone outside Paris.

She took a taxi to Benjamin's apartment in Montparnasse. He had told her he would be working at home that day. He buzzed her up; she left her luggage on the ground floor. He answered the door in an old sweatshirt and jeans, his hair wiry and wild, his glasses tipping slightly and his blue eyes crinkling at the edges as he smiled at her. Sarah dropped her purse, reached her arms around his neck, and hugged him tightly. He lifted her face to his and kissed her with so much longing and passion that her knees went weak and she forgot everything except the feel of his body against her own.

"I miss you already," he said.

He retrieved her bags and after setting them in his entry they did forget everything else that late summer afternoon except how much they wanted each other, their two lanky bodies entwined in Benjamin's bed, in his high- ceilinged bedroom littered with books and papers and clothes, the clothes they had been wearing tossed among them. They made love, holding on as if they might lose each other if they did not.

"I have to call Julie to let her know I'm in town," Sarah said, lying with Benjamin afterward. "Will you join us for coffee?" she asked him, dialing Julie's number.

"No," he said, turning on his side to face her. "I have much work to do."

When Sarah made the call it was clear that Julie was upset. She didn't want to meet Sarah just then. She had told Michel about the rape earlier that day and, according to Julie, he couldn't handle it. He had left the apartment very upset. Instead of coffee, Sarah invited Julie to join them for dinner. Julie declined but agreed to lunch the next day.

"Will you be all right?" Sarah asked.

"I think so," said Julie.

"You have my cell? The one I've been using in France?"

"Yeah. I've got it."

"Call me if you want to talk," said Sarah.

Benjamin and Sarah returned to L'Etoile, the restaurant where they had dined when they first met. This was the final weekend it would be open before closing for the remaining weeks of August, like so many of the good restaurants in Paris.

Sarah asked Benjamin to order for the two of them—the main courses and the wine. After giving the order to the waiter, Benjamin inquired about Sarah's plans.

"Are you sure this is what you want?" asked Benjamin.

"The duck in Cabernet sauce? I think so," said Sarah, teasing him. She looked radiant, her skin reflecting the unmistakable glow of a woman well loved. She wore a black sleeveless dress with a ruby-colored shawl over her shoulders. Antique diamond drop earrings, passed on to her from her grandmother and saved for special occasions, sparkled at the sides of her face.

"You know I am not speaking about the food," said Benjamin.

Sarah lifted her wine glass to her lips and sipped slowly. "Since when do we get to do everything we want to do?"

"How long do you think you will be gone?" he asked, trying a different tack.

"Gone? I've been gone *here*," Sarah gestured ruefully. Ask anyone in my family."

"Julie thinks this too?"

"Julie is young. A mature woman has obligations," Sarah knew she sounded cold. Nothing was coming out like she meant it.

"Mature. Obligations. Merde! I love you, Sarah! This afternoon—I've never loved you so much."

She placed her hands on the table, palms up. He responded by taking them in his own. "I love you, too," she said.

Benjamin registered surprise. "You say this now for the first time. Why, Sarah? Is it because you are leaving me?"

"No," she said slowly, "because it's the truth. Though I don't know what good it does to say it."

"Je t'aime, je t'aime," he repeated.

The waiter appeared with their dinners and they let go of each other's hands.

Over coffee, Sarah told Benjamin she had agreed to return to work within two weeks. It was hard for her to think about any of it right now but she didn't tell him that. She didn't want to sound like she had no life, no meaningful work even if that was the way she felt. On the other hand, how many people got to live out their dreams? Or even dreamt them? A vineyard in Provence? Spending the rest of one's life with a charming French law professor? Impossible, she concluded. A fantasy.

Benjamin told her he would need to make a trip to the U.S. soon. "I've mentioned my son, Phillipe, the one who teaches at the University of California?"

"Yes."

"He and I own a town home together in Berkeley. We bought it years ago as an investment. It has appreciated a good deal since then. In any case, I called him this week when I learned about a vineyard property. Henri informed Michel that a property on the road to Saint-Remy is for sale. It has an old, very small farmhouse on it—not as lovely as Pauline's but one with possibilities."

"How wonderful," she said.

"I would need to raise some money to buy it. I can do this only if we sell the place in Berkeley. My son, he is agreeable and said he would take his proceeds from that sale and share the cost of the vineyard property. He will make the investment with me." Benjamin stopped to sip his coffee. "He said, however, I must promise two things..."

Sarah watched him, deciding his was one of the most appealing faces she had ever seen. "And they are?" she asked.

"First, I must promise to come and visit him soon and meet my first grandchild—a boy named after me. I have only seen pictures. The child is barely one year old and already he is walking! If Marie were still alive, we would have made the trip by now."

"Of course," Sarah said. "Marie..."

Benjamin cocked his head, then went on. "And second, "Phillipe says I must invite him and his family to taste the fruits of our first harvest—the first wine made from the grapes planted in our vineyard. That would be, perhaps, three years from next fall if everything goes well."

"It sounds very exciting," said Sarah.

"It will not be unless you agree to be a part of it."

"As I said before, it's your dream, not mine."

"It *could* be yours," he said. "It could be ours."

She wanted right then never to leave him. But, she had to go home. She *had* to. "I know," she said. And as she said that, the tears that had been welling up in her eyes spilled onto her cheeks and her smile was full of sadness and longing.

The following morning, Sarah showered, dressed, and ate breakfast with Benjamin. Neither one spoke much. Benjamin did the breakfast dishes while Sarah finished packing, then worked for an hour while she read the paper and wrote some last-minute e-mails. Soon, it was time to leave.

"I could take you to the airport later," he offered.

"No," she said, "that's not necessary."

"Je comprends." I understand, he said.

She wondered if he *did* understand the unspoken part, the subtext. That she had to do the rest of this alone—her life apart from him. Or did she? It was only one of the questions without answers waiting for her back in Los Angeles.

They embraced in front of his building with the taxi waiting. A wind had come in from the north; it was unusually gray and cool for late July.

"I'll call you when I land," she said.

"I would like that," he said, lifting her face to his. Her eyes filled with tears but she said nothing more. His glasses tilted on the bridge of his nose as he kissed her softly. Sarah watched him as the taxi pulled away from the curb. She felt around in her bag for some Kleenex while craning her neck to see if he would turn around before the black lacquered door of the apartment house slammed shut, but he did not.

# 32

Sarah and Julie met for lunch in a small, noisy restaurant in Saint Germain that Julie had chosen. They both ordered salads but Sarah had lost her appetite after a few bites and sipped a glass of Chablis while Julie recounted the events of the past evening.

"Michel came home soon after you and I talked last night," Julie began. "I thought he would. He's a fantastic human being. He was upset when I told him about *that guy*, you know? I don't know, Michel thought things like that only happened to trashy girls. That's why he walked out. Like, it made him crazy."

"I can see that," said Sarah.

"Then, when he thought about it some more he was just angry it had happened to *me* and he was worried that I might never be happy or normal because of it," Julie said, becoming more and more animated.

"Hmmm," Sarah said.

"So, we had sex."

"Really?"

"Yes! Do you want details?"

"No, of course not," said Sarah. "But I would like to know how this ends."

"It's complicated, but it turns out we are better friends than lovers. I'm not really ready for a relationship. Meanwhile, he wants to settle down and have a family."

"How did you leave it then?"

"Well, I've decided to move back to New York—as soon as this workshop is over."

"What would you do there?"

"Mom, why do you always have to second guess me?"

"I'm sorry. I just want you to remember how you felt about it when you left. New York hasn't changed, I expect."

"But *I* have," said Julie. "I'd begun to self-destruct, after the rape. Then I met Tammy and a lot of other people and you invited me here and I met Michel and he thought I was beautiful and he encouraged me to think about acting again in a serious way!" Julie stopped to catch her breath. "So, I called my old roommates in New York—you remember that the person they found to sublet my room is leaving in September?"

Sarah nodded and sipped her wine.

"Well," Julie continued, "the timing is perfect. I plan to go back and get a job—any kind of a job—and apply to the MFA programs at Columbia and NYU next year. I mean I'll be 26 by then, and that's pretty old but—well, what do you think?"

"Twenty-six is not old, sweetie," Sarah said.

Julie took a long sip of Coke through a straw. "This way I'll be able to save some money and then apply for student loans when the time comes."

"It sounds like you've really thought this through," said Sarah. "I might be able to help out as well."

"That'd be great."

"I said, 'might'. We'll have to see," Sarah said, signaling for the check.

"How—uh—is Benjamin?" Julie asked.

"Well, it's complicated," Sarah said, and they both laughed and then let it alone.

Sarah had left her luggage with the restaurant's manager. He helped her carry it out to the curb after she paid the bill. Julie waited with Sarah until they were able to flag down a cab to take Sarah to Charles de Gaulle. Sarah was to stay at the airport Hyatt that night as she had an early flight Sunday. They gave each other an affectionate hug on the busy sidewalk.

"Give Grandma Claire a kiss for me," said Julie.

"I will," said Sarah. "Take care, sweetheart."

꿍꿍

"Welcome home," said the Customs agent at LAX. Sarah located her bags and moved swiftly through the U.S. passport line for international arrivals. She stopped at a kiosk and sent Benjamin an e-mail saying that she had landed safely, and would call him in a few days.

Too quickly, she was deposited into the hazy light and bad air of Los Angeles in August. She decided to take a cab to Santa Monica. One last indulgence before getting back to the real world, she thought

Sarah gave the cab driver directions to her mother's apartment and then leaned against the cloth seat. The cab was littered with empty coffee cups and a plastic water bottle, forgotten in haste.

Claire had come home mid-week and was doing well after the two transfusions. Becca had flown back to Chicago after getting Claire settled in her apartment. Claire's color was good and her breathing less labored, Becca had said.

"Where'd you fly in from?" the young driver asked.

"Paris," said Sarah.

"I've never been out of California."

"Would you mind if we didn't talk? I'm quite tired," she added, not wanting to be rude.

"Sure. These long plane rides...no problem," he said, merging onto the San Diego Freeway.

The cab driver pulled up to the white high rise on Ocean Avenue. "Here we are lady," he said.

She paid the cab driver and let him help her with her luggage. The doorman in her mother's building buzzed upstairs then rode with Sarah in the elevator, carrying her bags to apartment #1202 where Asya and Claire waited in the doorway.

Sarah felt as though she had been away for years instead of eight weeks. Claire looked thinner but all right, Sarah was relieved to see. She was not sure how her mother had perceived her absence; only that she hugged Sarah for longer than usual.

Asya had made up the sofa bed in the den. She was anxious to show Sarah some recent photographs of Claire and herself celebrating Claire's birthday. Asya was not young, perhaps only ten years younger than Claire.

Claire beamed at Sarah. She seemed particularly happy and weary in the way one is weary after waiting for something and it finally arrives. She reached to push Sarah's hair out of her eyes with a trembling hand.

The next day Sarah began her search for a short-term furnished apartment. She had stored the Honda in Claire's garage. It did feel good to get behind the wheel and drive a car that was familiar to her. Maybe this was all for the best, Sarah thought, as she parked in front of the first building.

Her attitude changed as soon as she saw the apartment and as she viewed the next several ones—all plain vanilla apartments with no character. She couldn't imagine cooking a decent dinner in any of them on their electric ranges and microwaves. The agents or owners would point out all the modern conveniences while Sarah envisioned Mas de Lumiere with its beamed-ceiling kitchen, the black enameled gas stove with heavy iron grates, the fresh herbs cut from the garden she tended with Henri and the cherry preserves from Pauline's orchard. Everything seemed surreal—the pastel colored stucco buildings, the cranky traffic, the singed air. What was she doing here? She asked herself as she drove back to Claire's. It was as though the last two months had never happened.

She placed a call to Asya telling her she would be there in time for a late lunch. Did Asya want her to pick anything up on the way? No, Asya told her they had eaten at 11:30 and that Claire was relaxing in her bedroom. Asya was just then washing the dishes.

Sarah wished she could tell her mother about Benjamin. She tried to imagine what Claire would say if she were able to. Her mother had been a practical woman—fussy, sometimes critical, careful in terms of money—but also a true romantic when it came to pursuing dreams, or loves. Sarah thought about how renting one of those apartments and going back to work at Kelton Hall felt like a huge step backward. Her head began to ache. It had been ages since she'd had a migraine. She hadn't had one since she'd gone to France.

Asya opened the door to the apartment and Sarah walked in, pushing the fingers of her left hand into her temple.

"You have headache?" asked Asya. "I get you aspirin?"

"Thanks," Sarah said. "I need to get something to eat and a Coke. Do we have any Cokes?"

"Coca-Cola we have," said Asya emphatically. "You sit and I get for you."

"I'll get it, Asya," said Sarah. She reached for a glass in the cabinet over the sink and filled it with ice. "How was your morning?" Sarah asked, diverting the attention from her pounding head.

"We talk, yes?" asked Asya. "Yes?"

Sarah made a sandwich and poured the Coke into the glass. She took them to the small dining room table next to the kitchen door and sat down. Asya followed her to the table.

"Well?" asked Sarah, taking a bite.

"Your mother, she no want to get dressed this morning. *This* is not normal," said Asya.

"Maybe she doesn't feel well," said Sarah.

"No, she's OK! She finally get dressed when I tell her we go out in the park. But then something else."

"What?" asked Sarah, aware of Asya's tendency to dramatize.

"After she get dressed she no want put on her jewelry—her ring and her necklace." Asya sat back in her chair.

Sarah ate the rest of her sandwich and drank some of the Coke. She swallowed the aspirin Asya had given her hoping the combination would kill her headache.

"Asya, what are you saying?" asked Sarah.

"I don't know. Just this, I'm telling you. You're her daughter. You should know!"

Sarah went into her mother's bedroom and sat down on the bed. Claire was dozing in her chair, her feet on an ottoman, dressed in pull-up slacks with an Oxford cloth shirt tucked into them—her post-stroke uniform.

Claire opened her eyes and smiled broadly at Sarah. "Hi," Claire said.

"Asya said you didn't want to get dressed this morning." Her mother shrugged her shoulders. "Are you feeling all right?" Her mother checked her watch.

"She also said you didn't want to put your ring on."

With these words, Claire said, "Oh!" and got up from her chair with some difficulty then shuffled to her dresser. She picked up the ring—a simple gold wedding band—and the necklace— a gold chain with a pearl every inch or so—and extended her hand with the pieces in it to Sarah.

"I'll help you put them on," said Sarah.

"No, no, no," Claire said shaking her head emphatically.

"I'm not sure what you want me to do with them, Mom."

Claire took a deep breath, sighed as she exhaled, and carefully placed the ring and the necklace back in the frosted blue dish on her dresser. Then she began a slow, halting walk toward her chair, the armrests fitted with cotton fabric covers Asya had sewn for her.

Sarah's head was pounding now. She lay down on her mother's bed and closed her eyes. Claire sat next to her and stroked her hair. Sarah felt her mother's cool, dry hand reassuring her—as she had done when Sarah was a little girl—that everything was going to be all right.

# 33

After spending a week looking at apartments and with only a few days left before returning to Kelton Hall, Sarah called Sharon in El Encanto to say she'd be coming on Thursday, as they had tentatively planned.

Sarah took the coastal route, passing the center of Malibu and heading north, remembering the last time she made the same drive. It was good to smell the ocean again. The salt air reminded her of the day in Cassis. She passed Ventura and the pier and the homes climbing the hills, then drove along the stretch of relatively pristine coastline between Ventura and Santa Barbara. She found a classical music station that was playing the slow movement from Brahm's Violin Concerto. Sarah thought of her mother, her father, of Julie and all she had been through, of David—of David sick, of David dying—and of Benjamin far away in France. Tears dropped down her cheeks. You take care of yourself, you try to be a good person, you work hard and still, still, things happen—tragedies even, because that's life and, as smart as we think we are, so much is a matter of luck.

The cell phone rang as Sarah approached Carpenteria, a quiet town just south of Santa Barbara that reminded Sarah of Provence.

"Hello?" Sarah said.

"Sarah, it's me, Asya. Something terrible it's happened with Claire."

Sarah swallowed hard. "What? She seemed OK this morning at breakfast."

"Yes, yes. She was fine. Ate nice breakfast. But she came to sit by me a minute ago and now her head falls forward. She no can talk. I think we need to do something. It's very bad. I'm so nervous."

"OK, Asya. OK. I'll come back. It will take me a little while though. Maybe you should just make her comfortable..."

"Sarah, we need call somebody. Go to the hospital. I never see this."

"Put her on the phone. Can you do that?"

Asya raised her voice. "No. You don't understand. She can't move. She can't talk. Her head fall to one side."

"Then call 911. Oh shit, they'll take her to Santa Monica hospital since it's the closest one and that's not where her doctors are." Sarah thought for a moment. "OK, Asya, all right. Call 911. I'll reach you at the hospital and I'll get there as soon as I can."

"Good you come. I call now."

Sarah managed her car into the right-hand lane and then off at the main Carpenteria exit. She found a gas station, used the bathroom and bought a Diet Coke from the vending machine. She did these things deliberately and with a calm that belied the turmoil she felt. Behind the wheel again, she followed the signs pointing South to Los Angeles.

It took Sarah only an hour and a half to return to Santa Monica. She found Asya and Claire in the ER. Claire looked like a frightened, caged animal—frail and wild-eyed in the hospital bed. She reached for the railing on the bed to pull herself up to a level from which she could escape but she fell back each time. Sarah stood beside her mother and held her hand. Claire gripped Sarah's finger tightly but there was no recognition in her eyes.

The young ER resident came in the room and told Sarah that her mother had had a brain-stem stroke. He began to speak directly to Claire, asking a number of diagnostic questions. Sarah interrupted him.

"She has aphasia," Sarah said. "She can't *talk* to you!"

"I know, but this is protocol," he said.

"Why?" asked Sarah. "It's cruel! Look, she was nothing like this before. We need to get her to Cedars-Sinai, to Dr. Blooming—that's her doctor. I have to call him." Sarah had her cell phone out.

"Hold on," the resident said. "She's not in any pain. And we can't move her yet. We need to make sure she is stable," he said.

"Can't you tell she's terrified? Can't you give her *something?*" Sarah spoke fast and eyed him furiously. He didn't know her mother.

Becca flew in the same night. It was midnight by the time the two sisters met at Santa Monica hospital. Claire was still awake and fitful. Sarah had not seen Becca in six months or more. They embraced each other.

"I can't believe it," said Becca. "I was just here. When I left, she seemed fine."

"I know. It happened very fast."

Once Claire was moved to Cedars and into a private room, she seemed to calm down. Perhaps it was the sedative, just enough to soothe the terrors, or perhaps it was the sight of her doctor—although she didn't seem to recognize anyone. But once she was tucked into her bed on the palliative care floor of the hospital, she closed her eyes. She looked as though she had fallen into a deep sleep. She never opened her eyes again.

Sarah called work to tell them she was back in the country and to let them know what was going on. She wasn't sure she would be in on Monday. She would let them know. Then she asked to be transferred to the dean's line.

"Hi Sarah," Carver said. "Welcome home! I bet you can't wait to get back to work. There's a lot going on."

"I don't know if I'll be in on Monday as planned," said Sarah.

"Why not?" he asked.

"My mother has had a brain stem stroke. I'm with her at Cedars. We've been told she's dying."

"I'm sorry."

"Thank you," said Sarah.

"Sure," he said. "Let me know if there's anything we can do."

# 34

Sarah and Becca planned the funeral for the following Wednesday. Julie needed time to get there. Sarah asked her to come and was relieved when Julie said she would. Mark had been driving home from a meeting in Milwaukee when he got Becca's call. He would catch a plane on Sunday.

Julie told the people in the drama workshop in Paris that she had a family emergency and would not be coming back. She planned to return to New York after L.A. Michel drove her to the airport and they parted as the best of friends.

Sarah was there when Claire died. Claire lay motionless in her bed, still on this earth though Sarah knew she was moving slowly—or at lightening speed—away from it. Sarah was in the room alone—Asya and Becca had gone to the Plaza Level for a cup of coffee—making a list of things she needed to do, when her mother's breath became less rhythmic and increasingly labored. Sarah put down her pad, dropping the pen on the floor, and hurried to the bedside. She felt her mother's head. She had been running a temperature and it was warm. It could have been seconds or minutes before Claire's breathing stopped. In those moments of profound mystery all signs of a struggle disappeared from her face. Sarah took her mother's hand; it was limp and soft and damp and she kissed her hand until tears covered it.

"I will always love you," she said.

Late that evening Sarah telephoned Benjamin. It was 6:30 a.m. in Paris. He answered with no sleep in his voice.

"It's Sarah," she said. "My mother died."

"I'm so sorry," he said. "It's very hard," he added.

"I didn't think it would be," she said, the tears coming like a wave. "I thought we'd already lost her."

"She is with God," Benjamin said.

"I think so," Sarah said, crying hard now.

"Cry, Sarah. It's OK," Benjamin said.

The chapel at Hillside Mortuary was filled with friends of Claire and Norman as well as Norman's former business associates and his golf buddies from the Club. There were, as well, old friends of Sarah's and David's—Sharon and Russell among them—even a few of Julie's close friends from high school. The service was neither too long nor too short. Becca spoke; Julie sang. Mark, looking younger and more relaxed than Sarah had remembered, made some poignant remarks. Sarah didn't. It was all right.

As Sarah left the private section of the chapel to get into the family limousine waiting outside, a hand tapped her on the shoulder. She turned around.

"Benjamin!" she said.

"I hope I am not intruding."

"What?" And she wrapped her arms around him. They stood like that until Becca walked by and said, "Sarah?" They pulled apart and Sarah dried her eyes. "This is my sister Becca and her husband Mark. I want you to meet my family," she said.

He shook their hands. Julie started to cry as he opened his arms to hold her.

Benjamin had caught the first flight he could book from Paris to New York, spent the night at the airport then flown on the 7:00 a.m. American flight to L.A. He traveled with only a carry-on bag, was able to breeze through Customs and had caught a cab to the mortuary having been informed by Michel of its name and address. He had stood with the crowd in the doorway but was still able to observe the entire service. Had Sarah stood to speak she might have seen him.

Benjamin quietly declined Sarah's invitation to ride with the family and didn't see Sarah again until after the interment service, held in one of Hillside's unexpectedly light and breezy mausoleums where Claire was laid to rest beside Norman, her husband of fifty-two years. Sarah thought of David, his ashes blown and scattered.

The gathering following the funeral was held at Claire's apartment. Sharon had organized it all. She ordered the deli platters and coffee cakes, the sodas and bottled water and the white wine. She also brewed plenty of hot coffee. Sarah, usually the one in control and able to entertain on a moment's notice, accepted the help with gratitude. It had taken all her strength to confirm the funeral arrangements with Becca and Mark, to place the obituary, to find something to wear.

Julie stood next to Sarah at the apartment and helped her mother and Becca greet the other mourners and thank them for coming. Benjamin walked in behind Ruth Sacks and Fanny Soboroff who had driven him to the house. He had stood near them at the interment and told them he was a friend of Sarah's from Paris. They wouldn't hear of him calling a cab and flirted with him all the way to Santa Monica.

"Sarah darling," said Fanny, embracing her.

"It was time," whispered Ruth into Sarah's ear.

Sarah had grown up with these two women, so much a part of her mother's life.

Then Benjamin was there, standing in front of her.

"Are you all right?" he asked, placing his hands on her shoulders. He had watched her from across the room while she greeted people.

"Mom, do you want some water?"

Sarah nodded. "Thanks, honey."

Benjamin led Sarah to the sofa in the living room. Julie brought a glass of water to her mother then returned to the others. Benjamin sat beside Sarah with his arm resting on the back of the sofa.

"You look tired," he said, "beautiful, but tired."

"I haven't slept much." Sarah admitted and drank the water.

"The ceremony was very moving," he said.

Sarah turned to him. "I can't believe you're here. It means so much to me."

"I was hoping you would say that."

Becca approached and sat down. "Julie tells me you have a son who lives in California," she said.

"Yes," Benjamin said. "In Oakland. I shall see him while I am here in California, although he does not yet know I am here. He and my daughter-in-law have a one year old baby, you see. I am a grandfather."

"Congratulations—uh—" stammered Becca.

"Benjamin," Sarah said.

Becca nodded as she stood up. "Benjamin, yes."

Benjamin rose from his seat. "My sympathies," he said as Becca walked away. He sat down and looked at Sarah. "After you called to tell me what happened I could not think about anything except seeing you. This is not an inappropriate thing I have done?"

"No, Becca is just upset. It has nothing to do with you. And I'm sorry I'm so quiet. I feel light-headed."

"You must eat something then. I will bring you something," he said, rising.

"Thank you," she said.

Benjamin stayed with Sarah while she tried to eat a turkey sandwich. He also declined her invitation to join the family for dinner that evening. He said he would call her in the morning then slipped away while she was talking to someone else.

The family dinner was quiet. Asya kept getting up to retrieve things. Gifts she had given Claire. Photographs.

"Here's one from the park. Your mother, she loved the park. And here, in the spring? You remember, Julie and Sarah here with Claire and me? Ah," said Asya. "I can't believe it."

Becca looked at Sarah. They would always be sisters, the look said, her bittersweet smile acknowledging the enormity of what had happened. Mark got up to put on water for tea.

Asya looked as though she remembered something else, something she believed to be important. "Wait!" she said and went into the bedroom. She came out holding the ring and the necklace.

"You see," Asya said, "she *knew*. Your mother, she knew. She try tell you—*so*. Now, you take them," she waved her outstretched hand first at Sarah then at Becca. When neither daughter reached for the jewelry, Asya sat back down, looking weary and older, her lipstick worn off, her mascara smudged beneath her eyes. "Claire, she was tired," Asya said.

# 35

Sarah and Julie were to spend the night at the apartment, Becca and Mark at a nearby hotel. After Mark and Becca left, Asya insisted on cleaning up the dinner dishes. Sarah and Julie collapsed in the living room.

"You were terrific today, honey. Really. It meant so much to me that you flew here all the way from Paris," said Sarah opening her arms to Julie. Julie lay down on the couch with her head in Sarah's lap. Sarah stroked her head.

"Benjamin is in love with you. You know that, Mom?"

Sarah looked down at her. "Benjamin's lonely," Sarah replied.

"Is that how you want to explain it all away? His wife died a long time ago. He's an attractive, intelligent man." She closed her eyes, shook her head, and then said, "And what's wrong with being lonely? You were lonely before you met him. Michel told me there's been a ton of women who've gone after him," said Julie. "But it's you he's in love with. You." She lifted her head and turned and then sat up to face Sarah. "What are you doing Mom? He's a great guy."

"I'm not doing anything. There's nothing to do. He lives in Paris."

"So?" said Julie, not letting up.

"I don't know. Grandma just died. I don't know anything."

"Look, Mom. I'll stay here for a few days but then I have to go to New York and get my life together. You don't have to stay in California. Grandma's not here anymore. Neither is Daddy.

I'll be in New York and that's almost as close to Paris as it is to L.A. Anyhow," Julie said after a minute, "I'd much rather visit you in Paris."

"Benjamin wants to retire and leave Paris and buy a place in Provence. He wants to grow grapes and make wine. He asked me to do that with him."

"See? I told you."

"He's kind of a dreamer."

"What's wrong with that?" asked Julie.

Benjamin called in the morning to say he was on his way to Oakland to visit Phillipe and his family. He would return to L.A. before flying back to Paris.

A week after the funeral he called again to say he was near the apartment in Santa Monica and asked whether he could come by to see Sarah and perhaps take a walk. She hesitated, not knowing why.

"Just a walk," he said in a clear, firm voice.

Benjamin and Sarah walked in the Palisades Park. They walked all the way up to San Vicente Boulevard and sat on a bench and looked out at the ocean. A thick fog was receding from the coast and the hills of Malibu were visible in the distance. Small groups of older men and women walked up and down the park—men in front, women behind. Other men and women—elderly, slow-moving—set up folding tables, preparing for an afternoon of cards and gossip.

On the walk they had talked about Benjamin's visit, about how his grandson resembled Phillipe, and about the sale of the townhouse. Sarah told him she had decided to take off another two weeks before returning to Kelton Hall. There was quite a bit of work involved with settling Claire's estate. Then they sat for a while without saying anything to each other.

"My son, he says I should fight for you," said Benjamin, interrupting the awkward silence between them.

Sarah smiled. "He did?"

Benjamin nodded. "See that?" he asked.

"What?" Sarah asked.

"Those couples. There. There." He pointed, then he took Sarah's hand. "I want to grow old with you, Sarah."

"There are no guarantees," she said.

"No," he kept hold of her hand, "we both know that. But I need you, Sarah. I want you to be my wife."

Sarah's eyes filled with tears as they kissed and held each other on the bench, the old women staring, chattering.

"All right," she said quietly, surprising herself, her eyes meeting his.

"All right?" he repeated.

"Yes," she answered. "Yes!"

He stood up and pulled her close. They kissed again and again and then, arms snug around each other's waists, they walked through the park overlooking the ocean, walked back to the tall white apartment building where Sarah's mother had lived.

༄༅

One of the things Sarah observed as she began the process of mourning Claire's death was that the disappointments—the list of grievances both imagined and real—that had spanned a lifetime simply evaporated. What remained was the undeniable experience of her mother's love. It had been the same with David, though his death had been more of a physical shock and the void his absence created less bearable. There had been more denial, more anger. But still, now, she could hold on to the best parts of their marriage and let the rest begin to fade.

The word 'profound' kept coming back to Sarah as she and Benjamin walked together that day. Profound: death and sorrow, the way love stirs the soul, the resilience of ordinary people. Sarah witnessed it in Julie and her recovery from the dual traumas of the loss of her father and of her innocence; in David during the final stages of his illness; in Claire as she adjusted to an altered reality; in Benjamin as he risked his heart again and now, unmistakably, in herself. For the chance at joy lies not in the guarantee of fulfillment but in the renewal of hope, tempered by missteps, lifting us toward the light.

www.ingramcontent.com/pod-product-compliance
Lightning Source LLC
Chambersburg PA
CBHW031306120626
46554CB00001BA/309